Stone Cottage

Maighread Mac

Cover Art:
MLC Designs 4U

Publisher's Note:

This is a work of fiction. All names, characters, places, and
events are the work of the author's imagination.

Any resemblance to real persons, places, or events is
coincidental.

Solstice Publishing - www.solsticepublishing.com

To: Paul

Stone Cottage
By
Maighread MacKay

Thank you so much for your encouragement & support. It means the world to me. Love you Maighread.

~ 3 ~

This book is dedicated to Sue Reynolds, teacher and mentor extraordinaire, without whose help it never would have been written. Thank you for your encouragement, advice and belief in me.

"There are more things in Heaven and Earth, Horatio, than are dreamt of in your philosophy."

— *William Shakespeare, Hamlet*

like a bird's wings trapped by the cage of her ribs, fluttered in her chest. She leaned her head against the cold glass and clenched her fists. Taking deep breaths to try and calm herself, she flattened her hands on the window.

"He's fine," she said. "I know it. Oh, Will, where are you? I need you so much. Please, please come home. Everything will be all right once you get here."

Tears coursed down her cheeks. The old dog, sensing her unease, leaned into her leg and began to whine. Absentmindedly, she reached down to stroke his head. She would just wait. Wait for as long as it took for Will to come home.

Wait...wait...wait, her mind chanted to the ticking clock in the hall.

Tick...tock...tick...tock...tick...

Chapter One

*R*ebecca jolted awake, every nerve ending on fire and screaming in panic. Icy sweat poured down her. Her heart was pounding so fast it felt like it would explode. She tried to take a deep breath, but couldn't. Absolute terror consumed her mind and body causing her to shake uncontrollably. The urge to run pulsated through her body and it took everything in her not to cry out. Gradually, she became aware of her surroundings and the palpitations slowed.

"Breathe," she told herself. Finally, she was able to take one lungful of air. Then another. Her breathing and heart settled into a normal rhythm.

Waking up in a full blown panic attack was the worst feeling in the world. When the attacks had started over a year ago, she had been terrified of going to sleep for fear that either she wouldn't wake up at all or she would, but in the midst of an attack episode.

"Oh, God," she muttered to herself, tears slipping from her eyes and following the now familiar path down her cheeks. Hot, seething anger consumed her. "No, damn it. I'm not going there again. I won't, I won't, I won't," she chanted while pounding her pillow.

She sat up and put her head in her hands. So frustrating. It had been months since her last attack. Her life was getting back on track. As a senior executive in the company her great-great grandfather founded, she was eager to make up for the time lost while ill. Now she realized the darkness was always hovering in the shadows ready to pounce. This morning was a reminder of how debilitating and draining the episodes could be. Wearily, she pushed herself into a standing position. The room morphed into a topsy-turvy landscape that threw her as she stopped the car in front of the building and stepped out. The warm rays of the sun enveloped her and the house in a soft cocoon. It felt as if she was being wrapped in loving arms that were welcoming her home. She had no name for the feeling it evoked. Premonition? Déjà vu? Not quite. Something stronger. Deep in her gut, she knew this house. In her mind's eye she could picture every nook and cranny, from the dusty attic to the cold basement. There was a feeling of security and family, a sense of laughter, giggles, sadness and tears. *Here I am,* her heart sang. *I'm home.*

Not understanding her reaction, she tiptoed a little closer to the house. It was very old. It looked like pictures she had seen of field stone houses built in Ontario in the 1800's. It was two storeys, with two long windows on each side of a central door. Above each set of windows was a dormer that Rebecca sensed were windows to sleeping quarters. Recessed back from the main house on the left was an addition with a smaller entrance. In her gut she knew it opened into a mudroom and beyond that, the kitchen. Since the cookery was on the left, it made sense that the dining room would be behind the windows on the left side of the main house. The windows on the right probably looked into the parlour, as it would have been called in its time.

Her feet crunched on the gravel as she crept up to the kitchen side of the house and peeked in a window. The property appeared to be abandoned.

Odd. No one seems to be here, but the house is clean so it's not completely deserted. I wonder where the owners are.

Since no one appeared to be around, she decided to explore a little further. She walked around to the backyard. A small herb and vegetable garden tucked behind the kitchen now lay abandoned and desolate. Looking up she could see three windows on the second floor. Circling the house, she spotted an old carriage house that had been turned into a garage. Beyond it was a greenhouse. Thistles and other assorted weeds had grown right up to the structure. Some of its glass panes were shattered. An abandoned bird's nest cascaded from the top ledge of the door. Loving flowers, she walked past the barn, to the greenhouse. She reached into her purse for a tissue and leaning on a window sill rubbed the grime from one of the intact windows. Cupping her eyes with her hands she peered into the interior.

Long tables she sensed once held beautiful flowers were aligned in rows down the centre of the room. Flower pots, covered with cobwebs, were lined up on the worktable at one end of the building, waiting for the gardener to come back and fill them with life. A rusted assortment of gardening tools was stacked near the worktable. Removing her hands from the window and turning away, she saw a formal garden. Many of the perennials had long ago gone back to their wild state. Here had been a rose garden and over there the wildflowers. She paused and knelt down to touch the soil and caress the new shoots beginning to sprout.

I wonder whose hand planted this. Look at the variety. It must have been beautiful. David would love it. It would make him happy to bring it back to life.

Gazing in the distance, she noticed a small hill. Climbing to its summit, the sunlight dappled the landscape as it sloped away from her. Shielding her eyes, she saw a large pond with a willow tree on its bank at the bottom of the hill. The edge of a wooden bench peeked from the other side of the tree. As she observed the scenery, a pair of geese with four goslings waddled through the tall reeds and set sail onto its glassy surface. A soft breeze slid like a silk caftan over her body. She took in a deep breath and released it, letting a calming sense of peace cascade over her.

"Like I told Maddy, I found this forlorn little pony wandering around the barnyard and she looked so sad. I knew a pretty little girl that would love her and make her happy, so I brought her here. See, they're friends already. I couldn't very well leave her by herself now could I?"

"No, Grampa, no. She's needs me. I wuv her. Can I keep her, Momma? Pwease?"

"Wandering around the barnyard you say," she said teasingly. "Well, I imagine she would be disconsolate without a companion and that would never do, would it, Grandpa. You promise to help take care of her?"

"Oh, yes, Momma. I wiw take the best care of her," said the child, bouncing around in circles.

"Hmmm...I guess we can keep her for now, but we'll have to check with your Papa later."

"How about we get you up on her back and go for a walk," said the man.

"Oh, yes, pwease."

The man lifted the child onto the pony's back and they walked around the pond, the dog racing ahead and then running back to join the group. It was a happy sight and Rebecca was so engrossed in the scene that she felt her heart melt.

The man spoke. "One day, Maddy, I'm going to buy you your very own big horse. Then you and I will ride, just like your mother and I did."

"Grampa," giggled Maddy. "Funny man. I haf my own horsie. See?"

"Yes, my sweet, Nelly is all yours, but she is a small pony. I'm talking about when you get to be a big girl. You will need a bigger horse and Grandpa will get you one. Okay?"

"Okay. I wike horsies. I wike doggies, too. I wuv Thor."

"Thor is a pretty special dog. Maybe we should ask your Momma if we could get you your very own puppy. What do you think?

"Oh, yes, Grampa. Wet's ask Momma. A new puppy. Yes," cried Maddy clapping her hands. "This is the bestest day ever."

The man lifted the child from the pony's back and she ran to her mother, throwing her arms around her legs. Her mother picked her up and the little girl said.

"Momma, guess what? Grampa told me we could get a puppy for my very own. Can we, Momma, pwease?"

The woman turned to the man.

"A pony and a doggie? You know Will and I will be having more children. She's not going to be lonely like I was, Papa."

"I know my dear but every child needs her own horse and dog, whether or not they have brothers and sisters. Besides, I can't wait until we can ride together like we used to. I'm not getting any younger, you know, so I want to start her early. It will be just like old times with you, me and Thor racing across the fields."

"Ah yes. They were very good times. It would be good for Maddy to have her own dog. How about we wait 'til next summer for the puppy. Will this be from one of the litters at the stables?"

"Yes, my dear. Stella, will be turning three and we're going to breed her the next time she goes into heat. I'm thinking of Roman for the father. He's a grand fellow and I'm interested to see what they would produce together. Maybe you would like to come home when she has given birth so that you and Maddy could pick out which one you want. I can keep whichever one you choose until you are ready for it to come home with you. How does that sound?"

"Perfect."

Slowly the light faded and the scene once again became the quiet pond with the goose and goslings swimming contentedly. Coming out of her reverie, shudders coursed through Rebecca's body. *What was that?* "Get a grip, lady. It was just a hallucination. The grave made me fantasize about who the people may have been. That's all. Just my mind playing tricks on me. I am going walk away from here and forget all about it."

Chapter Three

*S*traightening herself, she got up and started walking back to her car. As she passed the abandoned greenhouse, she stopped, sniffing the air.

That's odd. I smell the fragrance of chocolate mint. Where'd that come from?

As she looked into the ruins, a shaft of sunlight illuminated one small section of the room. Rebecca gasped unable to move. Hanging over a trestle table in the far corner was a single basket of Stanhopea Oculata, an orchid. One of her father's favourites. From the bottom of the basket hung several inflorescences with their weirdly shaped, purple and white-spotted flowers. Her body was enveloped by a sensation of enormous love and loss. Heat formed in her throat, cascaded through her stomach, down her legs and out the bottoms of her feet, leaving her weak and shaking. Raising her hand to her mouth, she cried out, "Daddy!"

He so loved his orchids. She used to think he loved them more than her. She remembered seeing him in his own conservatory last summer. He told her that he was purchasing a new orchid.

"It's a Cattleya lueddemanniana, 'Crownfox Goliath'." he said. "Cost me a fortune and can only be purchased from the Florida owners, but it's well worth the trouble, if it's as good as they say. It's supposed to have a spectacular fragrance. Just wait 'til O'Hara gets a load of it. His eyes will pop right out of their sockets." He was so excited he was rubbing his hands with glee. The twinkle in his eyes spoke volumes. She knew he was looking forward to the next juried show where he was sure he would beat his old rival.

Her heart broke a little more as she placed her forehead onto the glass and sobbed.

Doris had not seen or felt a thing. Rebecca mumbled something incoherent in reply.

She didn't see anything. I'm just spooked from what happened before.

Fear clutched at her heart, but she stuffed it down deep inside. Determined to explore further, Rebecca straightened her shoulders, marched across the hall and ascended the staircase. From the landing in the middle of the stairs she could see a hallway to her right running the width of the house with doors leading to what she presumed were bedrooms. After ascending the rest of the stairs, she saw a door on her left. Turning the knob, she pushed in open and peeked in. It was large and contained a bed, dresser, a couple of bedside tables with lamps, a window seat built into the dormer of the front window and a writing table. Good. No weird mist. Everything felt normal. Letting out a deep sigh, she thought, *Silly woman. It's just your nerves.*

Feeling a little calmer, she turned and walked down the hall to the first room. As she approached the room, her hands started to shake again. Alarm bells were going off in her head and uneasiness snaked down her spine. Entering the room, she gasped and bit down on her fist to stifle the tears that wanted to flow.

Oh, my God. This was a baby's room.

The mist was here and an image of the room as it had been over one hundred years ago overlay the modern furniture.

There's a crib, rocking chair, bookcase, and the mural of a pony painted on the wall.

Rebecca felt dizzy and, groping for support, lowered herself onto a solid bed. Tears poured down her face. The mist dissipated little by little, until the room was ordinary again.

Damn, that scared the hell out of me.

Panic clawed its way up to her throat from deep in her belly. The urge to run screaming as far away from here as she could consumed her.

I'll call Cissy from the car and have her meet me at the house. She'll know what's going on.

Closing her eyes and clenching her fists, the mania gradually subsided. Standing up on shaky legs and walking around until she was steady, she exited and descended the staircase. Hearing the vacuum, she composed herself. Doris's back was to her as she entered the parlour. She scanned the room looking for any mist and let it out a satisfied sigh when there was none. Before taking a step, she caught movement out of the corner of her eye. When Rebecca turned her head to the window she saw a young woman dressed in a flannel nightgown with a shawl wrapped around her shoulders, looking out the glass. The lady whirled and locked eyes with Rebecca. It was the same girl she had imagined by the pond, only she was different. Instead of the laughing mother, this woman's eyes were filled with a deep and haunted sadness as tears streamed down her cheeks. The same dog that had been in Rebecca's dream was seated at her side. The spectre was stroking its head. The two of them were as real as either Rebecca or Doris. Icy chills plummeted down Rebecca's body. Her hand rose of its own accord and clutched her chest. Letting out a whoosh of air, she slumped into the doorframe. In that moment the apparitions vanished. Shaken to the core, Rebecca was in full blown panic.

That's it. I'm outta here, now.

"I'm leaving now," she hollered over the noise of the vacuum.

"Had a look around did ya? Well, it was nice meeting ya. Hope to see you again sometime. If you're really interested in this place, talk to Murray Addison at the Realtor's in town. He's got all the lowdown on it and could probably get you a real good deal as the owner's want to sell quick-like. Hope I didn't spook you too much with all the talk about ghosts and everything. It would be real good to see someone living here again. Just needs to be spruced up a bit. You have a nice day now, eh?"

Rebecca turned and ran out of the house to the car. She climbed in, grasped the steering wheel and sobbed hysterically.

What the hell was that? The ghost? Impossible! They don't exist. I've lost my mind. Oh, God, I really need Cissy.

Still she couldn't deny what she had witnessed. There had been a young woman and a dog in the front room! The same duo she'd seen at the pond. Rebecca's body tingled like a thousand volts of electricity had passed through it. Her teeth were chattering and she was frozen to her core. Reaching for her purse, she grabbed her emergency bottle of pills. Taking one, she turned on the car, cranked up the heat and waited for the meds and the heat to kick in.

Chapter Five

*S*ilence. After all of the ruckus that afternoon, Stone Cottage was again enveloped in stillness. The leaves rustling intermittently in the afternoon breeze were the sole murmur that could be heard. The house was once again shrouded in the mists of time. The lone occupant of the home was speculating about what she had seen earlier. Victoria Anne McBride was in her usual place by the window. To her, it was still 1875 and the house and contents appeared the same as they had then. She had not seen or talked to anyone in one hundred and forty years - caught in an endless loop of fear, regret, and longing - but she didn't know that. Time meant nothing to her. As far as she was concerned, it had only been a couple of days since her parents had left and she was alone. It had startled her to turn from the window and see a woman around her Mother's age enter the parlour. That lady seemed shocked to see her as well, but she ran away before Victoria could talk to her.

I wonder who she. She looked terrified. Maybe she didn't know about Thor and is frightened of dogs? Why else would she run away? I wonder where she went. She just disappeared. I looked out the window, but she was gone. I'm so confused. Where is Will? I wish he would come home. Everything will be all right then. Where are you?

Walking over to her favourite chair she sat down, pulled up the quilt, snuggled in and closed her eyes. Dreams took her back to her first encounter with Will.

Bang, Bang. Bang.

What is that noise?

Her brain fogged with sleep, Victoria couldn't tell if the noise was real or part of a dream. Annoyed at being awakened, she tried to recall what she had been dreaming about. Smiling, she remembered. She had been galloping across the meadow on Athena's back with Thor at her side. Head down low at the side of the horse's neck, the wind had lifted her hair and sent it streaming from the back of her head. An immense awareness of jubilance and power burst from her heart. She was queen of her universe; an Amazonian Goddess in her own private world.

There it was again.

That infernal banging!

Well, there was going to be no going back to sleep with that racket. How dare someone call her back to her miserable reality?

Victoria Anne angrily threw back the covers and stomped to the window. Throwing back the curtain, she was about to call out when she froze at the sight in the garden. Her heart leapt into her throat and she gave a little gasp. The noise was being made by the most handsome young man she had ever seen. He was tall, with dark black hair. When he turned his head a straight nose and strong chin were revealed. His hammer was held precisely and almost delicately in hands large and rough. Strong arms used the tools to cleave the small boulders. The well-defined muscles in his back rippled with each blow. Busy repairing her father's stone wall, he had not seen her. She stepped back from the window, and peeked around the curtain. Mesmerized, she watched as he carefully chipped away at the rock. She thought about his hands caressing her skin and how those quivering muscles would feel under her exploration. Appalled at her thoughts, she backed into the centre of the room. Who was he? He must be one of the Masons whom her father had hired to repair the stone fence that surrounded the estate.

I must meet him, but how?

She paced the room trying to think. The maid had been in her room earlier to replenish the water in her pitcher and to bring in clean towels. Washing, she hurried to the armoire to pick out some clothes.

What will I wear? I can't let him know who I am or he won't talk to me. The dress I wear for the stables. Perfect. That way he may think I'm a servant. This will be fun.

Smiling to herself, she dressed, combed her hair and looked out of the window again. Yes, he was still there. Crossing to her door, she opened it slowly and peeked out to make sure that none of the servants were in the hall. Her mother would be in her drawing room and her father would have left for work. Creeping down the hallway she quickly descended the back stairs, ran out the back door and was in the garden in a wink. Wiping her hands on her dress, Victoria sedately walked to the fence. Her heart was galloping as fast as Athena in her dream. With her tongue stuck to the roof of her mouth, she clasped her hands to keep them from shaking.

Hearing someone approach, the young man turned and looked at her. Victoria returned his gaze. His eyes were dark sea-green. Staring into them she fell into a deep abyss of mystery and desire. Never had she seen eyes like his. A molten liquid formed in her belly and spread heat and warmth throughout her body.

He quickly stood up and gave her a slight bow. "Good afternoon to ye."

Released from her trance, she stuttered her response. "Hello. I saw you working and I was wondering who you are and what you are doing?"

"My name is Will McBride. I've come to fix the fence for Mr. Smythe-Stratton." His voice was fascinating. It was quite low, but had a soft burr and a wonderful lilt to it, almost as if he were singing his words.

"Do you live around here," she asked?

"Not too far. I live with me Da at the moment, but I'm building a stone house on a piece of property I have about two hours away. And ye are?"

"Oh, I'm sorry. How impolite. My name is...ummm...Annie. I live in this house."

"Okay, ummm...Annie. Do ye work here?"

"My mother works here and I stay with her," she replied crossing her fingers behind her back.

"It's time for me lunch, Annie. Would ye care to sit and talk with me while I eat? It would be pleasant to have company for a time."

"Oh, I would like that very much, Mr. McBride."

"Please call me Will. Ye didn't gie me your last name. What am I to call ye?"

She smiled at him. "Since you have suggested that I call you Will, you may call me Annie."

He smiled and made an exaggerated bow to her. "My pleasure, Miss Annie."

Victoria giggled. They walked to the shade of an oak tree in the garden. Will spread out his lunch and they began to talk.

"Were you born here...ummm...Will?" she asked ducking her head and blushing profusely.

"Aye. Me family's from Scotland. Me Da and two older brothers came out to work on Fort Henry in Kingston in '35 and stayed there until it was finished in'37. They decided they liked the new country and moved around a bit until they found this place and settled down. Da got one hundred acres from the government and once he had built his own place, he sent for me Mum and me other brothers and sisters. Two of 'em, plus meself were born here. I was born in '48. I ha' four brothers and four sisters. I'm the youngest. We are Kendric, Aindreas, Brid, Dara, Dafydd, Anwen, Ian, Fiona and me, Uilleam, but I'm called Will. The first five are all married and have a lot of children between them. We're a noisy bunch and full of opinions, so Sunday dinner is pretty lively. Da taught me all he knows about building things from stone and I love it. I get to work outdoors and with family. Da's getting on now and slowing down a bit, so me brothers and I will take over the business soon. Me Da split up the land amongst us boys, so we each have twenty acres and twenty acres for me Mum and Da. I'm building a house on me property. It's a pretty good life. What about you? Any brothers or sisters?

"No, I don't have any brothers or sisters. I had a little brother, but he died, so there's only me now," she said softly.

"Och, I'm sorry. I dinna mean to upset ye."

"That's okay. It was a long time ago, but it still is very sad. It's pretty lonely at times, so it's nice to talk to someone," she replied, lifting her head and smiling at him. "So, tell me all about your family. What's it like to grow up with so many people?"

Will started to tell her about his family and they spent the next hour laughing and talking about all sorts of things.

"Well, I really must get back to work. It's been lovely talking to ye, Miss Annie. Maybe ye could come again sometime?"

"I should like that very much, Will."

Will helped her get up from the ground and they walked to the back door. She turned, and giving him a sunny smile, waved before slipping in the door. Looking around warily to be certain no servants were near, she made her way up the back staircase and along the hall to her room. Her heart was beating loudly when she shut the door and leaned against it.

She had done it. She had actually spoken to him...Will.

He's so handsome. I could have stared into his eyes forever. And his voice, it was musical and lilting with a soft burr. I just had to close my eyes and I could see the mountains and heather of the Highlands waving in the breeze. The stories he told. It must be so much fun to have songs, laughter and people who love you.

told anyone else. Tha gaol agam ort (I love you), but you're probably right. I would have been completely tongue tied if, when we first met, ye introduced yerself as a Smythe-Stratton."

Releasing her hands, Will turned to Jonathan. "Sir, I would like permission to court yer daughter with the understanding that I would make her my wife. I have a very good trade. The home I was building has been completed. I love yer daughter with all me heart and will take very good care of her. May I have yer approval?"

Jonathan smiled at Will and stuck out his hand in offering. Will smiled back and shook the older man's hand.

"Since Annie seems to have a special place in her heart for you, I will give my consent on one condition. You will keep this affair quiet for the time being until I prepare Annie's mother. She has her heart set on Annie marrying into high society, whereas I, on the other hand, would rather she make a match of her own choosing. When the time is right, we will invite you to the house so that we can get to know you. Annie's still young, so there's no rush. If all goes well, we shouldn't have to wait too long to have a wedding."

"Thank you, Papa, thank you," exclaimed Annie as she threw her arms around her Father and kissed his cheek. "You won't be sorry, I promise. I love Will so much. We will have a wonderful life together and you will have lots of grandchildren to bounce on your knee."

"Well, first we have to convince your Mother. As for grandchildren...that can wait. I'm in no rush to see my girl leave home and belong to another man, as much as you say you love him."

"You'll always be my first love," she whispered as she smiled at him. "I will never really leave you as we will always live in each other's hearts."

Jonathan eyes misted over and he coughed into his hand to hide his emotion. "I think it is time for tea, my dear, and I shouldn't like to keep your Mother waiting. Say your goodbyes to your young man and come into the house."

"Will," said Jonathan tipping his head towards him.

"Mr. Smythe-Stratton," replied Will. "Thank ye, sir. I will take good care of Annie."

"I will hold you to that, son. My daughter is the most precious thing in my life and if you have won her heart, you best take very good care not to bruise or hurt it in any way or you will answer to me." Jonathan turned and walked to the front of the house.

"I must go, Will, but I will be back tomorrow at the regular time. I am so happy that you know the truth and you still love me. I love you more than I can ever express. I promise we will be very happy and ours will be a wonderful life."

Will took her face in his hands and gently kissed her lips. Her very first kiss. Overwhelmed, she could not breathe. She had dreamed of this moment her whole life, but could never have imagined how delicious it would feel. When it was over, Will needed to hold onto her or she would have slipped to the ground. As it was, she was quite tipsy when she opened her eyes. As she had learned from many, many years of practice, she quickly suppressed her emotion until she was calm. You would never suspect that this had been the most earth shattering moment of her life.

"Mo chiall (my darling)," whispered Will stroking her cheek gently. "I will see you tomorrow."

Annie picked up her skirts and ran to her Father who had waited for her. Laughing she threw her arms around him and kissed both his cheeks. "Thank you, Papa. You have made me so happy. I love Will with all my heart and I can't wait to be his wife. This has been the most wonderful day of my life. Now, let's go and get that tea."

completely off balance. Reaching for the bedpost to gain her equilibrium, she hung on tightly while the room righted itself.

What the hell? Oh, God, I'm going to be sick.

Her mouth was bone dry. The ensuite appeared to be at the end of a long tunnel.

"I can do this. I can do this," she recited over and over.

Feeling like the hoofs of a Clydesdale horse had attached themselves to the end of her legs, she pushed away from the bedpost and shuffled forward. With fierce concentration, Rebecca made it to the bathroom and turned on the light. Swishing out her mouth with cold water then, opening the medicine cabinet, she took out the Lorazepam. Holding back the tears that threatened to overwhelm, she swallowed a tablet.

Thank God for the meds. I'm fine. Just a minor setback.

Stripping off her soaked night gown, she turned on the shower and stepped in. Warm water cascaded down her body. Rebecca let the discouragement and fatigue flow down the drain with it. The fragrance of her shampoo enveloped her, bringing back memories of a time when she was full of life and looking forward to each day.

After drying off, Rebecca slipped into her jeans, favourite T-shirt and a pair of low heeled shoes and thought about what she wanted to do. A soft spring breeze wafted into the bedroom to caress her nostrils with a bouquet of lilacs and new-mown grass. It was a beautiful day. A few clouds, like cotton batting, spread across an azure sky. The birds chattered to each other, busy with their early morning chores. Feeling the meds kick in, she thought about going for a drive. Before her illness, climbing behind the wheel of her car, pedal to the metal, feeling the wind on her face gave her such a rush. Exploring back country roads looking for treasures was one of her favourite thing to do. Now, not so much. Driving had been one of the first things to go after the panic attacks began. Recently, though, she'd been practising to get back into the swing of handling her Porsche Spyder and much of her confidence had returned. She thought back to the first car that she had loved. It had been a sparkling red BMW Z3 convertible roadster with deep-leather white upholstery that her father had gifted to her when she went off to McGill for her MBA. Remembering that vehicle, she thought about her Dad and their special relationship.

Ah, Daddy. I love you so much. You'll never know what you mean to me and how I miss you. I've always felt safe and loved with you in my life.

That car had been so much fun. Reminiscing about the times that she and Cissy would take off on their own, Rebecca laughed. The two of them. No destination in mind. Cruising along, singing at the top of their lungs, and enjoying the freedom she'd always felt behind the wheel of a car. Longing for some of that freedom, for the last couple of months she'd been tossing around the idea of finding a cottage or cabin of her own where she could find solitude. Right now everyone in her circle was so worried, she felt smothered.

I love everyone, but I need to get away where no one is hovering, afraid I'll splinter at the slightest provocation.

Snapping out of her reverie, she determined that's what she would do. Go for a long drive and see what was for sale. With her heart feeling a little lighter, she skipped down the stairs to the kitchen. "Mrs. Brown, I'm going out for a little while. It's such a lovely day, I'm going for a drive."

"That's wonderful Ms. Wainwright. Some fresh air will do you good. Enjoy yourself and I'll let Mr. Connacher know if he should come home before you've returned."

"Thank you. Tell David I have my cell. I should be home for supper."

Stopping in the front hallway to get her purse and keys, she glanced in the mirror. The woman looking back was beginning to resemble her old self. Smiling, she headed out the front door.

Chapter Two

$\mathcal{R}$ebecca spent the morning driving aimlessly around the countryside. Trees were sprouting new foliage and within days would be in full leaf. Birds were migrating north and red winged blackbirds had returned from their winter home. All nature was coming alive. She was alive! For the first time in ages, she felt free and happy. This was the perfect medicine to shake off her previous hysteria. Rolling down the windows, Rebecca cranked up the radio and be-bopped her way along the highway singing at the top of her voice. She searched small towns and hamlets looking for the hideaway where she could be herself with no pressure. Nothing caught her attention. There were some lovely places for sale, but they didn't tug at her heart strings. After stopping for a leisurely lunch, she got back into her car and headed home. She was pleased that she had followed her instinct. Feeling better, she let her mind go. Not really concentrating on where she was, she passed a side road near Port Perry. As soon as she had passed it something nudged her to turn around. She frowned.

Hmmm... that looks vaguely familiar, but I don't remember being here before.

Following her gut feeling, she backed up and started down the road. At the crest of a hill, she spotted a narrow path almost hidden by the trees. There was a dilapidated 'For Sale' sign hanging askew by the edge of the road. It was barely visible in the tall grass. Feeling almost giddy, she turned onto the path to see what could possibly be at the end. As she crept along the overgrown track, tall trees on either side arched over the road casting it in dark shadows. Goosebumps stood up on Rebecca's arms and made her shiver. The lane gave way to an old stone house with a circular driveway. The sun broke through the clouds

"Oh, Daddy, I miss you so much. Why did you leave me? I feel so alone." She blinked a few times and rubbed her eyes. The sunlight faded and with it the strange vision. Her strength spent, she leaned with her back against the greenhouse and slumped down to sit on a large rock. Her mind reeling, she sat with her head in her hands thinking about her father and their tumultuous relationship. How she adored him. She had always been his 'Princess', but at the same time, she never thought she quite measured up to her older brother, James. She wanted her Dad to be proud of her accomplishments and to believe in her abilities as a competent business woman. Unfortunately, he was old school when it came to women and their place in society. They were adornments to be loved and pampered, but not equal to men. One of his most often used quotes came to mind...'Women should be happy with their homes and families and leave the real work to the men'. Rather than earn her place in the executive suite, she felt it was given to her because she was his daughter. Constantly striving to win his approval and always afraid she had failed, she thought back to one of the last conflict they had about it.

Rebecca sat in the empty board room, the well-manicured nails of her right hand clicking out a staccato rhythm on the mahogany table in front of her. She looked at her watch and frowned. Slamming her portfolio shut, she pushed back her chair and strode out of the room and down the hall to the CEO's office.

"Janine", she said bristling with anger. "Where's the team from Chandler Industries? We were to meet this morning at 11:00 in the main board room? I've been waiting for the last twenty minutes."

"I'm sorry Ms. Wainwright, but the meeting was brought forward to nine o'clock and they finished a while ago."

"Why wasn't I informed of this change?"

"I...I'm sorry, but I was told not to bother you," Janine replied.

"Not bother me? This is my project. I need to be informed regarding any and all changes on this deal. Is that understood? Do not...I repeat...do not ever let this happen again."

"Yes, Ms. Wainwright."

"Is he in there?"

"Yes, ma'am, but he doesn't want to be disturbed."

"Well, he is going to be whether he wants to or not. Don't buzz him. I'll announce myself."

Rebecca turned and marched directly into the CEO's office. Slamming the door behind her, she faced the man seated at the large desk in front of her. Charles Wainwright looked up as she entered, a smile lighting up his countenance. He stood and walked toward her. He was a tall man, impeccably dressed in a dove grey Armani suit. His silver hair glistened in the light and his cobalt blue eyes twinkled behind steel rimmed glasses. He exuded power, but it was tempered with a kind demeanor.

"Rebecca, my dear, this is a nice surprise. You look upset. Now, what's troubling that pretty little head of yours?"

"Father, I understand that you changed the time of the meeting this morning and didn't bother to inform me."

"Well, I knew you were visiting the building site this morning. Chandler called and asked to move the meeting time up. What was I to do?"

"You should have called to let me know of the change. This is MY project and I should have been in that meeting. I would have rescheduled the inspection of the building site."

Charles eyes turned to ice.

"Rebecca, I'm still the CEO of this company and I will not have my decisions challenged. We needed to have their signatures on the contracts ASAP. There were a couple of minor changes. James was here and he filled in for you. I'm sure he'll be happy to give you an update."

"James was there? What was my brother doing in my meeting? Doesn't he have enough to do without taking over my projects?"

"Enough. It was a good opportunity for the team from Chandler's to meet James. I wanted him to get to know the group so that if we run into any problems they'll be able to contact him if you're not available."

Feeling the usual tingle of shame flow through her body, Rebecca instinctively looked at the floor. Tears of frustration were held in check by sheer determination. If only she'd been born a boy, they wouldn't be having this conversation. It was really no use badgering her father about his style of doing business. She raised her eyes and looked at Charles.

"I apologize if it looks like I'm criticizing you, but you know how much my projects mean to me and I would appreciate it if you would let me handle them without bringing in James. It undermines my credibility with the staff when it appears that you do not value my work. It also makes me feel that I am only an EVP because I'm your daughter, not because I am good at what I do."

"I don't know where you get that idea. I would never have given you your position unless you earned it. Now, why don't you run along? The project has been satisfactorily completed for all intents and purposes. Just a little mopping up to do. Go on out and buy yourself a new dress. Or better yet, go home and take those granddaughters of mine to visit their grandmother. She would love to see them and the two of you could have a nice chat. Everything has been put to bed and you can relax for a while."

Rebecca closed her eyes and sighed inside. The pain in her right eye was starting to pound and she knew another migraine was headed her way. He just didn't see how his actions belied what he said. James would always be informed of everything connected to one of his projects. Just once she would like to be appreciated for what she did not who she was.

"Father, I do not wish to go and buy a new dress. As for taking the girls to visit Mother, this is Thursday and she has her bridge club. I only want you to understand how important my work is to me and to respect me for it. Please do not exclude me from important aspects of projects that are my responsibility."

"Yes, yes, my dear. Well, we'll talk about it later. I have a conference call in a few minutes and I need to prepare. Come, give me a hug. I can't have my beautiful girl be seen leaving my office upset, now can I?"

Rebecca walked forward to her father and was embraced in his strong arms. She smelled his favourite cologne and her heart melted. She could never stay mad at Charles for long. She loved him so much and just wanted him to see how good she really was. Was that too much to ask?

"That's my girl. Show me the lovely smile that lightens my heart every time I see it." Charles ended the hug patting Rebecca's shoulder. He lifted her chin with his hands and looked deeply into his daughter's eyes. Rebecca smiled at her father and kissed his cheek.

"One of these days, I'm going to drag you kicking and screaming into the 21st century, Mr. Wainwright."

"Yes, I'm sure you'll try. Now scoot."

How she missed those strong arms around her. "Life isn't the same without you. I'm trying to get better, but I don't know if I will ever be truly happy again. I wish you were here."

The sun broke through the clouds and she sat for a little longer soaking up the warmth. Finally, she rose and walked to her car. She climbed in and sat for several minutes bewildered and saddened by what she had experienced. Questions whirled about in her mind.

What the hell is going on? What is this place? I've gone crazy. Completely over the top. Either that or my meds aren't working properly. I need to see Dr. Holden again. Perhaps she has some logical explanation.

The tableau at the pond. *Weird.* She had never encountered anything remotely like that in her life. She never had hallucinations, visions or seizures, so what happened? The orchid in the greenhouse. It could have been a trick of the sunlight playing off the glass, but she didn't think so. Cissy said her father would make his presence known to her one day and what better way than by an orchid. Orchids meant love, beauty and strength.

Was it a sign as Cissy said? Is he telling me that he is still watching over me? That's nuts. He's been gone for over a year. Why now? Why here? What's this place got to do with me?

Chapter Four

*R*ebecca waited until her emotions were under control, then started the car.

I need to go home.

She took one more look at the house.

It's beautiful. Exactly what I've been looking for. I need to come back again, but next time I'll bring Cissy, so if anything happens she'll be able to help me.

As she manoeuvred her car around the circular drive, she heard another car approaching the house. She watched as a decrepit mini minor came into view and stopped. The driver, a middle-aged woman dressed in blue jeans and tank top, with long brown hair tied up in a scarf, exited her vehicle. Rebecca turned off the engine as the woman approached. She opened the door and climbed out.

"Hi," said the woman. "My name is Doris Barkley. I'm the caretaker of this place. I wasn't expecting to see anyone today. Can I help you?"

Steadying herself Rebecca replied. "Hi, my name's Rebecca. I would like to know more about the house and grounds."

"Well, the owners moved away to the States a while ago and they are eager to sell and have it off their hands. What else do ya want to know?"

"Do you know any of the history of the house?"

"I've lived around here all my life but I only know the gossip about what went on. I heard tell it was built by a William McBride way back in the 1800's. He was supposed to have been a stone mason. He, his wife and little girl lived here for a while. The story is that he went to Toronto for work. While he was gone the Mrs. and the baby got sick or something and died. Anyway, I've been told they're buried down the hill, by the pond but I don't know for sure. You won't get me going down there. This place is spooky enough without giving myself nightmares. Imagine burying folks in your backyard. Gives me the chills. I don't know much else, but maybe the Real Estate Agent could help you, if ya want to know more."

All the while Doris was speaking, iciness ran up and down Rebecca's spine and the hairs on the nape of her neck were standing as rigid as soldiers being inspected by the Queen. That was strange. She had never heard of these people. Were they the ones she'd imagined down by the pond? Only the man seemed quite a bit older and the woman had called him Grandpa in her dream, so she doubted he was William. It had to have been a daydream. It couldn't have been real, although the grave was certainly real.

"What happened after their deaths? Was the house sold?"

"Don't know much more. I did hear that William came home to find his family all gone. He didn't have much heart after that, but continued to live here awhile. He died a few years later and is buried with the McBride family in the old graveyard at the four corners. It's a sad story all around. It's said that one of their ghosts haunts this place, but I've never seen it."

"Really?"

"Well, if they do, I wish they'd clean up some. I still have to come out every two weeks to give it a scrub. Easy money. Since nobody lives here it don't get very dirty, but like I said, it gives me the creeps. I wish somebody would buy it so I don't have to come here no more. It's such a sad place. Well, I need to get started on my cleaning. You wanna come and see the inside?"

Rebecca felt her heart leap at the suggestion.

Would I like to go in? You bet I would. Should I chance it with all the weird stuff that's happened? Suck it up, Princess. The old Rebecca would have jumped at the chance to see inside. What could happen anyway with Doris here? Besides, ghosts DO NOT exist.

"Yes, I would like that."

Doris got her cleaning supplies out of the car. Walking up to the door, she set down her utensils, got out her keys and opened it. Stepping back to pick up her equipment, she allowed Rebecca to enter the house first.

A blast of cold, stale air assailed her nose as Rebecca stepped into the foyer. She shivered in the iciness that blanketed the front entrance and stomped her feet to keep warm. She looked around the vestibule which was large and square with a staircase leading to the second floor directly across from her. There were two doors, one on either side of the foyer that led to the other rooms on the ground floor. The hall appeared empty, but as she turned to face the door on her left, she saw an old grandfather clock shimmering in a grey mist. Her heart slammed against her ribs and started to hammer so loudly she was sure Doris could hear it outside on the porch. She shut her eyes and when she opened them again, the mist and clock were gone.

Oh shit.

Doris bustled past, not even noticing that Rebecca was rooted in place. She opened the door on the right.

"This here's the living room and that door over there leads to the dining room. I'll be in here, vacuuming for a while, so take your time and look around. Oh, yeah, the house was wired for electricity sometime awhile back and it's been kept up. We do have wifi out here, so you can hook up your computer and TV and stuff if you want to. Some people who have rented the place over the years have wanted to experience what it was like in the 'old days', so they haven't wanted a TV or anything. Nuts if you ask me, but then, it's none of my business."

Jonathan and Annie turned and walked back to the house and into the side garden where they found Will sitting on a large rock, with his head in his hands. As they approached he lifted his head. As soon as he saw Jonathan, he stood.

"Mr. Smythe-Stratton, sir," he said. "I'm sorry if Annie is bothering ye. She and I had a slight disagreement and she ran off. I tried to find her, but I didn't know where she'd gone. I hope she is not disturbing you, sir."

Jonathan smiled at Will. "Not at all...not at all. It's all right, my boy, although I think Annie has something to say to you."

Annie looked nervously at Will and then down at the ground. Her arms hung at her side and her fingers nervously plucking at her skirt. Clasping her hands together in front of her, she spoke. "I'm sorry for running away, Will, but I haven't been completely honest with you. You see, my name is Annie, but that is my second name. My first name is Victoria. I am really Victoria Anne Smythe-Stratton and this is my Father," she said extending her hand and placing it on her father's arm.

"What," stammered Will? "What do you mean you're not Annie? Why did ye lie to me? I dinna understand. Am I not good enough for ye? Do ye think of me as a joke?"

"No, no, Will, you're not a joke. That first morning I saw you in the garden, I wanted to meet you. I was afraid if you knew who I was, you would put a shield up between us and we'd never get to know each other. I needed a friend. I decided if you thought I was a servant, we could talk like normal people. Then I fell in love with you and I was scared you wouldn't want me because I lied."

Taking her hands, Will lifted them to his mouth. Placing a kiss on each he said,"Oh, Annie, mo ghraidh. How could I not want ye? I love ye. Ye took ma breath away the first time I saw ye. I've told ye things I've never

"I'm so sorry, but I can't. I do love you, but it's impossible. It's all my fault."

"What's yer fault? Why are ye running away? Please come back and talk to me."

Annie continued to run around the corner of the house. Blinded by tears, she did not see a man standing just outside the door. She crashed into him. He grabbed her arms and held on. "Please unhand me, sir."

"Annie, pet, it's Papa. What's wrong?"

Annie raised her head and looked into her father's puzzled frown. "Oh, Papa," she cried. "I've made such a mess of things."

"Now, now," said Jonathan, taking a handkerchief from his pocket and wiping her eyes. "I'm sure everything will be all right. Let's go for a walk and you can tell me all about it."

Taking her arm and tucking it into his elbow, he steered his daughter down the path to the lower garden. Once she had stopped hiccoughing and had gained control of herself, Annie started to explain to her father everything that had happened over the last few months.

"I would like to meet this young man," said Jonathan.

"Oh, Papa, you can't. I would be so embarrassed. I told him that my name was Annie and that my Mother worked in the house. He will know that I lied to him and will probably be angry with me. At first, I didn't want to tell him who I really was in case he wouldn't talk to me and then time went on, I...I...couldn't tell him I lied. Now I've spoiled everything."

"Yes, that is a problem, is it not? But, your name is Annie, that wasn't a lie and your Mother does work in the house - just not how you implied. Let's go face him together. If he is as upstanding a young man as you say he is, I'm sure he'll understand."

Chapter Six

*O*ver the next few months, she and Will met many times and she learned a great deal about his family, Scotland and the craziness of a large household. How he made her laugh. It didn't take long until she had fallen deeply in love. He became her life-line and she sought more and more time to be with him. Although she shared a lot about her own life, she couldn't quite summon up the courage to say that she was actually the daughter of the house. She was so afraid that he would never speak to her again if he knew that she was a Smythe-Stratton and his employer's daughter. She meant to tell him at the beginning of their relationship, but the longer she waited, the harder it became. He told her all about the house he was building and she longed to see it. She could picture it in her mind and knew that she would love the place with all her heart. How she wished that it was hers and that she and Will lived there together.

About six months after their first meeting, Will came to the garden as usual, he was very excited and pulled Annie into a secluded spot where he told her that he had finally finished the house. Now that it was done, he was in a position to offer for her hand in marriage.

"Ah Annie, mo ghraidh (my love). I have grown to love ye deeply, but I wasn't in a position to ask ye to marry me. Now I'm ready. Would ye do me the great honour of becoming my wife?"

Annie released his hands and stood up. She was shaking and crying. "Oh, Will, I can't marry you. I just can't." She turned and ran towards the house.

"Annie, wait. What's the matter? I thought ye loved me as well. Why won't ye marry me?"

When she thought of her own family and the coldness of her mother, her heart plummeted. Henrietta would never allow a friendship with 'the help'.

Why can't I have a loving and warm family?

With a bruised heart sore from her Mother's harshness, Will's talk about his family restored her soul. Like water poured onto a sea sponge, she soaked in every word. She could picture the scenes so well and her spirit revelled in the antics of the clan. The only other time she felt so happy and alive was riding Athena, with Thor racing alongside. Determination welled up in the core of her being. She'd have to be very careful no one spotted them and told her Mother, but nothing and no one would stop her from meeting Will. Those precious moments were hers to relive again and again in the lonely days ahead.

How delightful. I love this place. I feel so at home here.

She smiled, really smiled, for the first time in months. Absorbing the feeling of contentment, she walked down the hill towards the tree. As she got nearer to the water, she gasped. A sensation of vertigo assailed her. Her stomach clenched and she thought might throw up. She stopped.

What on earth?

Her uneasiness made absolutely no sense whatsoever. How could she switch from such peace as she'd felt a moment ago to this feeling of loss and heartache? She continued on cautiously. She approached the far side of the willow and peered around it. "Oh, my God," she gasped. There was an old tombstone tilting in the grass not far from the tree. Here the atmosphere was thick with pain, grief and loss. Making her way to the grave, she knelt down and gently rubbed the dirt from the marker. The epitaph read:

In loving memory of

Madeleine McBride

Beloved daughter of William and Victoria Anne McBride

Born January 27th, 1872 – Died August 8th, 1875

Aged 3 yrs 7 months

Victoria Anne McBride (Smythe-Stratton)

Beloved wife and mother

Born January 11th, 1852 - Died August 13th, 1875

Aged 23 yrs 7 months

May they find happiness in the arms of the Lord

There appeared to be a smaller mound beside Victoria's, but Rebecca wasn't sure if it was a grave or not. Clouds which had been threatening rain covered the earth and blanketed her spirit. Still feeling slightly dizzy, Rebecca's heart compressed in agony.

They were both so young. Madeleine was just a baby, her mother only twenty-three. But why are the graves here? They must be connected to the house somehow.

The ubiquitous tears that had been her companion for months, formed in her eyes. She had no idea why she was reacting this way. It was almost as if she had known them. As if they had been very dear to her, but that didn't make any sense.

She stayed with her hand on the stone, kneeling on the grave, lost in overwhelming sadness. She rose, walked over to the bench and sat down, the ache of loss and regret settling in the pit of her stomach. Who were William, Victoria and Madeleine McBride? Why were only Victoria and Madeleine buried here? What happened to William? Why do I feel so drawn to them?

The sun broke through the clouds and the world became quiet and still. As Rebecca sat, the scene in front of her changed. She still faced the pond, but instead of Mama Goose and her goslings she saw a young woman accompanied by a dog and a little girl about two years old. They were collecting wild flowers, dancing in the sun, blowing dandelion seeds, chasing butterflies and just being happy. Their clothing was vintage. *Early 1900's at least, perhaps even earlier.* The toddler laughed at the seeds floating in the air. As Rebecca watched, an older man leading a small pony approached the trio.

"Grampa," squealed the child racing to him.

"Hello, my pet. Look what I found wandering around the barn. She looked lonely, so, I thought, I know a little girl who would love to play with you. What do you think? Would you like to be her friend?"

"Oh, yes. Momma, wook Grampa brought me my very own horsie. Oh, I wuv her," she said clapping her small hands.

The woman approached the pair. "Papa, what have you done?"

waiting for him. He should have been home hours ago. Where was he?

She rubbed her arms hoping to bring some warmth back into them. Pacing the floor, she tried to restore the circulation to her legs. Cold, so very cold. Even though she was wearing her best flannel nightgown and had a shawl around her shoulders, she couldn't get warm.

She felt as if she was in a dream, with no sense of the passing of time. The darkness eerie and menacing. Even the familiar surroundings seemed off somehow, but her foggy brain couldn't place what was wrong.

As the woman stirred, the dog raised his head to look at her. She smiled at him. Her faithful companion. As long as she had Thor beside her some of the foreboding she felt slithered back into the shadows. Another loud crack of thunder made her jump again. The awareness of how alone she was increased as apprehension undulated up and down her spine. She pulled the shawl tighter across her shoulders.

"C'mon, Thor," she said. "Let's go see if Will's light is in the barn."

He got up from his comfortable place and padded across to where the woman stood. Victoria reached down and patted his ancient head. He looked up at her, tail thumping on the floor. Licking her hand, he nudged his head against her leg. Dog and woman walked to the windows and peered out at the storm.

The cacophony of the moaning wind and lashing rain concealed any sound of a horse's hoofs. She could see nothing, except the murky fog. No light. No Will. *Where are you?* Her anxiety escalated to new heights. Her baby girl was asleep upstairs, but she seemed to have been sleeping for a long time. Was Maddy sick? Victoria knew there was something important about the baby that she had to explain to Will, but she couldn't quite remember what it was. She needed her husband to come home to take her in his arms and tell her everything would be all right. Panic,

Prologue

*I*n the aftermath of the blinding flash, the darkness shimmered like liquid ebony. The wind ripped the leaves from the trees and tossed them aside. The rain slashed the windows of the isolated aged stone house.

Inside the dwelling, all was silent except for the ticking of the longcase clock in the foyer. The parlour to the right of the front door held a sofa placed in the centre of the room facing a large fireplace made of fieldstone. Two tall windows looked onto the lawn at the front of the house. Comfortable chairs flanked the fireside. A small table holding a glass lamp was located beside one of the chairs. A handmade throw rug covered the highly polished wooden floor in front of the hearth. An old dog lay asleep on the mat. With the shelves filled with books, the soft glow of the fire and gas lamp, and the comfortable chairs, the parlour had been warm and cozy in the gloomy night.

Victoria Anne McBride, the solitary human occupant of the room was curled up in one of the chairs, a blanket covering her and a book on her lap. A sonic boom of thunder shook the house and ricocheted around the room breaking the spell of silence. Startled, she surged from the chair, the eiderdown and tome cascading to the floor. She had been feeling warm and drowsy under the quilt but now realized there was nothing but cold ash left in the fireplace. The gas lamp on the table had burned out and the room was freezing. How long had she been there? She listened as the rain scratched the window glass like the long nails of a ghostly hand pleading to be let in out of the cold. Bringing her awareness back to the moment, she tried to remember why she was here in the parlour. Will. She had been

Chapter Seven

Victoria stirred in her chair. How she loved her husband. She missed him terribly when he was gone. This time it seemed like he had been away longer than ever. Her first kiss. It was so exciting. Thinking about it and remembering what followed made her giggle.

That was exciting, but nothing prepared me for what came later. All of my fantasies about being held in Will's arms pale when I think about what those hands and mouth did to me.

Then she remembered when her mother found out about them.

A few weeks after meeting her father, Will and Annie were sitting on the large rocks where they met for their usual lunch date. Annie was laughing at some remark Will made. A shadow fell over her shoulder and she turned to find her mother standing behind her with a frown on her face.

"Victoria, what do you think you are doing?"

Annie jumped to her feet, red faced with embarrassment.

I will not let her make me feel guilty. I have done nothing wrong.

Annie composed herself and clasped her hands demurely in front of her. She raised her chin and looked her mother straight in the eye. "I am having lunch with Will, Mother," she said defiantly.

"I am appalled at your lack of decorum. Sitting on a filthy rock, talking to the help without my permission. Come up to the house, young lady, and we'll see what punishment will be appropriate for this scandalous behaviour."

"No, Mother, I will not. Will is my friend and we will finish our lunch together."

Henrietta was shocked at her daughter's refusal to obey. "Victoria, you will do as I say or there will be severe consequences. Just who is this young man and why are you calling him by his first name? How long has this so called friendship been going on?"

"Mother, I would like to introduce you to Mr. William McBride. We met several months ago and have become friends. He and I have given each other permission to call one another by our Christian name. As I said, we will finish our lunch together and then I will come into the house and see you in your drawing room."

Henrietta pulled herself up into her most haughty posture and turned her attention onto Will. "Well, Mr. McBride, I am not at all pleased to make your acquaintance. If being with you has given my daughter these appalling manners, then you are not the sort of person I wish her to associate with."

Will smiled his infectious smile and nodded to Henrietta. "I am pleased to make your acquaintance, ma'am. Yer daughter is the loveliest person I know and I am very glad to call her my friend."

"Hmph...I bet you are. Trying to ingratiate yourself with your betters, are you? She has become very free with her favours I see, and I am not at all pleased". Turning back to Victoria, she said. "Since you have chosen to defy me, I have no alternative but to speak to your Father. He is in the study at the moment and unless you come with me right this minute, I will be going to him."

"No, Mother, I will not come with you. Speak to Father, if you must, but I will be staying with Will."

Henrietta gave her daughter a glacial stare that should have caused Annie to turn into an ice sculpture. She then turned on her heel and strode back to the house, her head held high and her back rigid. Annie excused herself from Will and followed her mother. She stood outside the study window so that she could hear what her parents said. Arriving at the study door, Henrietta knocked and proceeded to enter the room. Jonathan was seated at his desk and looked up as she entered.

"Hello, my dear. To what do I owe this honour?"

"Jonathan, I have come to speak to you about our daughter. I have just left her in the garden with the young stonemason you hired. I fear she has developed a tendre for him," fumed Henrietta.

"His name is Will and yes, she has discussed it with me," replied Jonathan.

"With you,and not her Mother? Well, I hope you discouraged her. She would be foolish to waste her future on one such as he. I have been looking at the various families of our acquaintance and can assure you that there are a few very good prospects. The Laings' and the Perrys' have sons a little older than Victoria, and with her dowry and their connections, I'm sure that she can make a brilliant match."

"But, she does not love any of them and is not interested in a brilliant match."

"What nonsense! Whoever marries for love? You know as well as I do that marriage is a contract. Love. What does that have to do with a successful marriage? What kind of life will she have with that...that...person? She will never be able to move in society, never be accepted in fashionable drawing rooms."

"Perhaps she will be happy."

"Nonsense. Do you think she'll be happy in some hovel without servants and people of her own class? Really, Jonathan, your flights of fancy never cease to amaze me."

"If a good marriage is to be judged only on making a 'brilliant match' as you put it, then ours certainly falls short of the mark. When we first married, I had high hopes that, although we didn't love each other, we would develop a deep caring and have a harmonious and happy life. That now appears to be impossible. This marriage has made you a bitter, angry woman and I do not wish that to happen to our daughter. Therefore, I will not stand in the way of happiness for her. If she and Will choose to be wed, I will give her my blessing. I would advise you to do the same if you wish any relationship at all with your daughter."

Annie thought about that day and what her mother had said as she paced the parlour in Stone Cottage.

Mother never did consider my happiness. A 'brilliant match' was all she cared about. It makes my blood boil to think of how little she cares about my feelings, or the man I love. I will never let her take away my happiness. Will is mine now and so is Maddy. Oh, she makes me so angry. She did everything in her power to stop the wedding.

* * *

Henrietta's horror at the man her daughter had chosen became more palpable as time went on. All of her dreams of marrying Victoria to the station to which she was entitled had vanished like the early morning mist on a hot summer's day. She continued to pick away at what she saw were Will's glaring detractions. To Annie, it felt like someone was constantly pulling at the scab on a heart trying to heal. One morning Henrietta called Annie to her sitting room. She looked at her only child.

"How could you be so impertinent as to associate with that young man? After all your father and I have done for you."

"Enough, Mother," she shouted stamping her right foot in anger. "I will not listen to one more word that you say against Will. I love him and I have chosen him to be my husband. If you do not cease your constant clamoring, I will go to the nearest judge and be married within the week.

I am over eighteen and am free to marry whom I will. Do not push me any further. If you wish to save face and have the lavish wedding you've been dreaming about, you will stop your criticism and be quiet."

"You are a child Victoria and an ungrateful one at that. Your Father and I have spared no expense to launch you into society, as befits a descendant of Dukes and Earls. Yet you besmirch your heritage associating with persons beneath your station. I really do want what is best for you."

"Will is not beneath my station, Mother. We are not in England anymore and titles do not matter here. He is a fine man and will work hard to make a good life for us."

"That's another thing, you have allowed him to call you by your first name. In my day, it was just not done. Are you purposely trying to humiliate me? Is this how you get your revenge for my supposed neglect of you? Oh how I wish your brother had lived."

Annie looked at the floor. This was not the first time she had felt her mother would rather have had her die and her brother live. She should be used to it by now, but each time she was reminded, she felt another small piece of her confidence break off and pierce her heart. Lifting her chin and straightening her spine, she looked defiantly at her Mother. "No, Mother. You do not want what is best for me. You want what you think is best for you and me. I do not agree with you. You despise Will because he is a businessman. My father is a businessman but you have never forgiven him for that, have you? Why did you marry him? You certainly don't love him and you've been miserable your whole married life. Well, I love Will and I intend to marry him. Will you please stop your incessant disparaging remarks? I do not wish to hurt or humiliate you, but I have never been interested in high society. I just want my own home with the man I love."

"Victoria, don't be insolent. It is none of your business why I married your father. These matters are not discussed with children. As grown up as you think you are, I am still your mother and demand some respect."

Annie sighed. "Yes, Mother. Can we please stop fighting and agree not to speak of this again? I would like to talk to you about wedding plans. You wish to have a lavish production to show to all your friends. I only wish for a small intimate ceremony. If you cease your constant complaints about my choice of husband, I will let you put on the wedding you wish. Can you agree to that?"

"I should hope that you would want me to be a part of your wedding. All right, I will say no more about the man you have chosen. I do have a few ideas about the nuptials you may want to consider, so let's talk about them."

Henrietta refrained from making any more remarks about Will, and in the days and weeks that followed she and Annie had a fragile truce. Once Henrietta realized that Annie wasn't going to change her mind, she resigned herself to the fact and threw every ounce of energy she had into making this wedding the grandest affair of the season.

Annie sighed. What a wonderful day it had been. As much as she was angry with her mother, she had to admit Henrietta had outdone herself to put on the most memorable wedding in the history of Briar's Mills. Her gown was the most spectacular confection she had ever seen and the wedding feast after the ceremony was so splendid that the villagers talked about nothing else for months.

Her wedding gown! She giggled as she remembered it. Henrietta had sent to France for the very latest in fashion and the garment the modiste created was quite mesmerizing. She thought about a gift that her mother had given to her. They had been in her room, preparing to leave for the church. She was shocked when Henrietta commented, "You look lovely, Victoria. I...I have a small gift for you."

Henrietta brought out a small box that she had in her pocket. She opened it and took out a necklace. It was a small circlet of diamonds with a drop pendant of a blue sapphire in a tear shape suspended from the centre. She placed it around Annie's neck.

"This necklace was given to the Duchess of Kent by her husband on the occasion of their marriage. It has been passed down to the eldest daughter of each succeeding generation on their wedding day. It was given to me by my mother the day I married your father and I have saved it to present to you on your wedding day. May you be happy in your new life."

How she loved that necklace. She had it put away in a special box for Maddy.

I will give it to her on her wedding day, as my Mother gave it to me. Even though we will have other children, she is my first born and it is for her.

Maddy. There was something about her that she should remember, but she couldn't quite grasp what it was. She turned back to the window looking for Will. Once he came home he would explain everything to her. She would just have to wait, but, oh, she missed him so much.

Chapter Eight

Rebecca, still shaking, drove away from the house. She found a small clearing in an alcove of trees and pulled over. She didn't want Doris to see her upset. Satisfied that no one could see her from the road, she waited until the meds had calmed her sufficiently. She picked up her phone and dialed Cissy's number. "Cissy, it's me. I'm in the car. Can we meet at my place in a couple of hours?"

"What's going on, are you okay?"

"Not really. I'm a mess and I need to talk to you about it. Will you be able to meet me?"

"Yes. I've got a conference call at eight o'clock, but I'm free 'til then. I'll just finish up some paper work and meet you at your place."

"That's great. I'll be waiting for you."

"Where are you? Are you sure you're all right to drive? You sound weird."

Rebecca snorted. "No, I'm not but I will be. I'm up around Port Perry just off Highway 12. Something weird has happened and I'm really rattled. I need to talk to you right away."

"Okay, I'll be there as soon as I can. You're sure you don't need me to come and get you?"

"No, I'm fine. Just hurry, please."

Rebecca hung up the phone. Her hands were still shaking. *Okay, breathe,* she told herself. *Long breath in, long breath out. Again. You've got to calm down so that you can get home. Think about Cissy. Remember the fun times. That first time you met and how unlikely your friendship seemed to be.* Rebecca thought back to that first meeting.

It was August of 1996 and Rebecca was on her way to McGill University in Montreal. After driving for hours from Toronto, she arrived at her destination. She had rented a small apartment in a charming triplex owned by a Madame Garnier. Madame was very particular about the class of her tenants and only rented the apartments to female students at the University. There were to be no loud parties and smoking was not permitted on the premises. Rebecca's flat was on the second floor and there was another apartment across the hall. She had learned that it was rented to a post-doctoral student by the name of Cecilia Walsh.

I wonder what she's like. I'm exhausted, just let me get upstairs to the apartment and have a hot shower. Then, food. Wonder if I can order in? My bed. Ahhhhh, my bed.

She climbed the stairs dreaming about her soft bed when she saw that the door to her apartment was open. *What the?* She pushed it open, only to find someone else was there.

"Excuse me, but who are you and what are you doing in my apartment?" she asked.

The young woman turned. She was petite. Her hair, the colour of daffodils on a sunny, spring day, was tied up in two dog-ear pony tails. Her huge, grey eyes were set in an elfin face that radiated with intelligence and humour. A turned up button nose that wrinkled when she laughed, danced in the middle of her face. Dressed in a peasant blouse and a long, wrap-around skirt, she wore no shoes on her dainty feet. She was holding what Becca recognized as a crystal on a string that she had been about to attach to the window pane. Rebecca could hear soft lilting music playing in the background. When the woman saw Rebecca, her eyes widened and her mouth turned up in a huge grin. Advancing toward her, she spoke.

"Hi, I'm Cissy. Well, actually, I'm Cecilia Walsh, but, I ask you, do I look like a Cecilia? I mean, Cecilia's are tall and willowy and oh, so sophisticated. Look at me. I look like a woodland Sprite. My Mom thinks I'm a changeling from the faery kingdom. Probably am. But, anyway, I'm not really a Cecilia...so I call myself Cissy. My Mom was enamoured of Cecilia Payne, the famous astronomer. Anyway, she was so hoping that I would be a renowned scientist and I guess, in a way, I am, sort of. I mean, I am going for my Doctorate in Pathology, so that's a scientist. Just not the kind my Mom was hoping for. But I love the mystery of life and death and how the body works, so Pathology it is. You must be Rebecca and your apartment is across the hall."

"My apartment's..."

Cissy laughed. "Across the hall. Madame Garnier said that we were to be neighbours. Are you related to the Wainwright's of Wainwright Industries? Wow, all those wonderful clothes. That must be why you're decked out so beautifully. Look at that dress, it's gorgeous. Me, I have no fashion sense at all. I mean, I look like a throwback to the 60's, but it's comfortable and I do like being comfortable."

At five feet eight inches tall, Rebecca felt like a giant that had stumbled into a munchkin land. Shaking her head to remove the cobwebs and fatigue, she replied, "Yes. I'm related to those Wainwright's. My Dad is Charles Wainwright, Chairman of the Board."

"Super, maybe you'll be able to help me spruce up a little. My Mother will bless the ground you walk on. She's a real stickler for 'proper attire'. Scares me to death sometimes. Oh well," Cissy sighed. "I guess I really can't keep looking like a hippy waif the rest of my life. But, I really, really do like being comfortable."

Rebecca had to laugh. Okay, not what she had pictured as a post-doctoral student, but Cissy was kind of endearing in her own quirky way.

"Tell you what," said Cissy. "Why don't you go to your apartment and get out of those travelling clothes, have a hot shower and get comfortable. Then we could meet in say an hour and grab something to eat. I've got to finish hanging these crystals, then I need to meditate for twenty minutes, but I can be ready in an hour. What do you say? I just knew I was supposed to bunk here this semester and now I know why. I was supposed to meet you. We're going to be great friends, I just know it."

Crystals, meditation, hippy waif? Whoa. Maybe we should take this slow and easy. Rebecca wasn't at all sure that they would become great friends, but a hot shower and some food sounded like heaven. It probably wouldn't do any harm to at least eat with her, so dinner with Cissy it was.

Chapter Nine

*F*eeling much calmer, Rebecca started the car and drove home. On her way she remembered how they their friendship had developed over the next few weeks. Although their schedules were different, they often had study periods when they would go to the local coffee shop to study, cram or just gossip. With her warm and nurturing nature, Cissy slowly helped Rebecca to loosen up. The first time Rebecca cracked a joke was marked with a high five and a cheer.

One Thursday, a few months after they had met, Cissy asked Rebecca if she could help her find an outfit for her parent's 30th wedding anniversary. She was fretting because her mother was one of Montreal's social elite and the epitome of elegance and grace. She deplored her daughter's style of dress (or lack thereof) and often expressed dismay over her choice of clothing.

"It's only a couple of weeks away and I really don't have anything suitable. My wardrobe is sadly lacking in my Mother's eyes and she would faint if I ever showed up in what I usually wear. I've been thinking of making some excuse not to go, but I would like to. Is there any hope that you might be my fairy godmother and transform this mouse into a princess?"

Rebecca laughed. "I was hoping you would ask. Now you're in my country. First thing...the hair dresser to get those locks looking sophisticated and sexy. I'll call Francois and get you an appointment; he's one of the best in Montreal. I've been itching to do a makeover for you. This is going to be so much fun!"

A few days later Rebecca and Cissy walked into Chez Nous hair salon. The wooden floor was set in wide dark-oak planks and to the left of the door was a comfortable lounge area with soft butter-cream leather couches. Vases of flowers and potted plants were placed in small niches recessed in the off white walls. Light jazz was playing through the in-house speakers. To the right of the door was a staircase leading to a product display area and the reception desk. Behind the reception desk were etched glass doors that led to the main part of the salon. Rebecca approached the desk.

"Hi, Anik. I have an appointment with Francois at one o'clock. Would you ring for him, please?"

"Mademoiselle Wainwright, how lovely to see you again. Certainment, I shall call Francois right away." Anik lifted the phone receiver and pushed a button. "Francois, Mademoiselle Wainwright est ici. Attend, s'il vous plait."

A few moments later a tall, slim man having blond hair with bright pink tips, came through the door and approached Rebecca. Taking her hands in his, he kissed both cheeks. "Mademoiselle, how delightful to see you again."

"Francois, I've brought you my guinea pig. Take very good care of her. I'm going to wait in the lounge."

"Absolutement, mademoiselle."

He took Cissy's hand and led her through the doors to his station. Seating her in his chair, Francois got to work and within two hours, Cissy got a look at her new hair. It came to just below her ears and fanned out from her head. The back was cut just below the nape of her neck. The front swept in long side bangs. Everything was light and fluffy and she looked more like a pixie than ever, albeit a very sophisticated pixie.

Taken aback, she could just get out a squeak. "Is that really me? I look so different. Wait 'til Becca gets a look at this. Thank you Francois, this style is stunning."

"I'm very glad you approve, mademoiselle. Let's go show Mademoiselle Wainwright the finished product."

The stylist led Cissy out of the main salon and into the lounge. Upon hearing the doors open, Becca put down her magazine and stood to see the new Cissy.

"Look at me...all sophisticated and grown up," she said with glee, twirling around so that Becca could see her new do.

"You look fabulous, dahling. See, I told you Francois was a miracle worker. I love the new cut. Thank you so much, Francois, for your assistance. The cut is lovely and really suits her."

Rebecca took Cissy arm and the two ladies strode out the door.

"Now, let's see about that gown. I've made an appointment with Madame Deschamps at her boutique on les Cours Mont-Royal. She's waiting for us."

"Of course you have," Cissy laughed.

Together the two friends walked down the block to an upscale couturier. Rebecca was in her element. They entered the premises. The atmosphere was hushed, as if they were in a fine art museum. Old money and exclusivity reigned supreme. Soft lavender carpet covered the floor and the walls were of an eggshell hue with lavender accents. Tea and small delicacies were offered to clients by assistants clad in muted lavender smocks. Classical music was playing in the background. Quiet elegance was the order of the day. Rebecca approached a young woman staff member.

"I'm Rebecca Wainwright and I have an appointment with Madame Deschamps. Please tell her we're here."

"Certainment, mademoiselle, I will get her for you right away."

A small woman, whom Rebecca thought to be in her sixties, approached from the rear of the boutique. Her white hair was fashionable styled and she carried herself with regal authority. She smiled.

"I am Madame Deschamps. You are Rebecca Wainwright, non?"

"Oui, I am Rebecca Wainwright. It's lovely to meet you Madame. I have heard a lot of good things about your boutique. I'd like to see the new line of fashion for McQueen, Versace and Valentino."

"Is this for yourself, Mademoiselle?"

"No, it's for my friend," she said pulling Cissy forward. "We need a gown for an evening function. Please show us what you think will suit."

Madame studied Cissy's face and shape, looking carefully at her eyes. She took note of her height and posture, measuring her until she felt satisfied that she knew which gown would be perfect for her. She clapped her hands and called, "Gizelle, venez ici rapidement." One of the shop attendants hurried to answer the call.

"Oui,Madame?"

"Gizelle, amenez-moi le Versace avec l'épaule dégagée dans le rouge et la tenture de lacet de Valentino dans le bleu royal. Oui, n'importe lequel d'entre ceux-là devrait faire joliment."

Ah, a royal blue Versace and a red Valentino. As Madame said, either of those should do nicely, thought Rebecca.

Gizelle scurried to find the items requested, returning with them in hand. Madame instructed Cissy to follow Gizelle and shooed them into a dressing room.

"Now we wait. I think you will be pleased with my choices."

In a few minutes, Cissy came out of the dressing room. She was wearing a long, sheath Versace gown in red. It fitted her slim figure perfectly and made her appear taller and very sophisticated.

"Turn around," instructed Rebecca.

Cissy did a little pirouette and stopped in front of the two ladies.

"What do you think," she asked?

"It's lovely. Very good choice, Madame. Now let's see the other one."

Cissy went back into the dressing room and returned in a few moments.

Rebecca gasped.

"That's gorgeous. How do you feel?"

Cissy appeared in front of them dressed in beautiful creation of royal blue silk by Valentino with an off the shoulder bodice, long flowing skirt that flared at the hem and was embossed down one side with lace embroidery. She was absolutely stunning.

"I feel beautiful, sexy... wonderful. For the first time in my life I feel like a grown up and desirable woman. This is the most exquisite dress I have ever seen."

"Perfect. Well, Madame, I think we have found THE dress. Please wrap it up and have it delivered to this address," responded Rebecca, handing Madame her business card. "Please put it on my bill." Turning to Cissy she said, "No Cissy, my treat. I've wanted to do this since we met. I'll need your help some other time and we'll be even then."

Cissy changed into her street clothes and the two friends exited the store in excitement and laughter.

"Now, on to the accessories. Shoes, jewellery, clutch. What a great day," sighed Rebecca.

"Thank you so much for your help and gift, Becca. Even though it was me who asked for your advice, I understand and appreciate your generosity. I will figure out a way to repay you that will be as meaningful to you as this excursion is to me. I wouldn't have known where to start without you. I love the dress. My mother is going to be thrilled when I show up wearing it. I hate clothes shopping, but this is a trip I'll never forget. What a fantastic day. I just knew we were meant to meet."

***

What a day that had been. Rebecca smiled to herself as she replayed it in her mind. Mrs. Walsh was thrilled with the new Cecilia. Cissy felt like the belle of the ball and the makeover was a huge success. Cissy and Rebecca sealed their friendship with what to Rebecca had been a routine shopping trip. It always amazed her that a simple act of kindness could bring such happiness to someone else. A few weeks later, late on a Friday afternoon this act was reciprocated and Rebecca was on the receiving end of Cissy's generous heart.

Chapter Ten

$\mathscr{R}$ebecca stormed into Cissy's apartment and slammed the door. Throwing her briefcase onto the table, she fell into the chair and threw her arms over her eyes. "Arrgh, I just don't need this!"

Cissy, sitting on her yoga mat in front of the window, opened her eyes and stared at her friend. Bringing her consciousness back to the room, she said, "What don't you need?"

"Any more stress. This day has been horrible. I woke up late, stubbed my toe getting into the shower, didn't have time for breakfast, just missed a cab and it went downhill from there. The last straw was when I went through my bag looking for my study notes for Monday's mid-term and they weren't there. I know I had them yesterday. I retraced my steps back to the lecture hall. I went to the office to see if anyone had turned them in. I've torn my apartment apart looking for them. I just can't find them. I've wracked my brain trying to remember where I saw them last. Think. Think. Think." She thumped her forehead with the heel of her hand.

"Why don't you relax?"

"RELAX!" shouted Rebecca. "What planet are you from? How can I relax? I need those notes. Some of us have to study for our exams and I can't do that WITHOUT MY NOTES."

"Becca, calm down. First of all, I know exactly where your notes are. You left them here on the coffee table when you were over last night. I was going to return them to you when we saw each other today."

They're here? Hallelujah, there is a God! I was sure I had lost them. What would I ever do without you?"

"Well, hopefully, we won't have to find that out for a long time. Meantime, I really meant it when I said you need to calm down. If you're going to be a big shot in your Dad's company, it would help if you can be serene and rational when you're with the old boys' club. Why don't you come to yoga with me? At least you could learn some breathing techniques to soothe yourself when you're about to lose it, and I know the postures will help ease the knots in your muscles."

Rebecca looked at her friend. Her mind registered Cissy's yoga clothes, her mat and the meditative soundtrack playing in the background.

"Yoga? Oh, my goodness, you were meditating when I came in, weren't you? I'm so sorry to have disturbed you. I guess I should have knocked."

"Well, that's what I get for leaving the door unlocked," muttered Cissy.

"But, honestly, Ciss, can you see me doing yoga? All that woo-woo stuff. I mean, no offense, but it really isn't me."

"I've told you before, it isn't woo-woo stuff. It's a way of consciously breathing and moving to bring harmony to your mind, body and spirit so you can get through this life relatively in one piece. It helps keep you on an even keel to face each day without getting upset at every little thing that happens."

"Humph. I don't get 'upset at every little thing that happens'. Do I? Well, I suppose I tend to react a little strongly when things don't go the way I want them to. What do you mean, 'breathing'? Everybody breathes. You kinda have to, to stay alive."

"Yeah, everyone breathes, but not consciously. The kind that calms the body. At yoga, you learn to still the mind by focussing on your breath. You helped me with the dress for my parent's party. Now, I would like to help you learn how to take control of your mind so you can quiet your emotions when you start to spin out of control. I really wish you'd come with me."

"Well, I'll see how my schedule is for next week. If I can get through the exam and if I find I've nothing else to do, I might try to go with you."

"That's great. Let me know how your week's going. I hope you can come with me. Now, why don't you let me get dressed and we can go and catch some dinner."

* * *

Checking her calendar, Rebecca realized that she had Tuesday evening open in the next week and decided that she would like to go to Yoga with Cissy. Maybe it wouldn't be such a bad thing to learn how to relax. She called Cissy and told her that she would be okay to go with her to class, if she was going.

Tuesday night the two friends packed up their gear and walked to the Yoga Studio. Rebecca could feel her nerves tingling and the knot in her stomach grow just a little tighter the closer they got to the studio.

Great! I come here to learn to relax and I'm wound up tighter than a spring, but I don't like this stuff. I'm sure everyone here is weird or nuts. I don't think it will work. Just get me out of here. She chuckled to herself. *Trust me to find a solution to a problem that only makes it worse.*

Walking into the building, Rebecca was pleased to find the yoga classroom was warm, bright and cheery and filled with about a dozen other people. A few were quietly laughing and talking placing their mats on the floor, while others were lying down ready to begin. Rebecca surreptitiously glanced at them. No one seemed strange or weird. In fact, she recognized one woman as the Manager of her bank and another man was the Vice President of a marketing firm she'd met at a fund raiser.

Hmmm, can't be all that bad if these people are here.

Cissy took her hand and led her to a young woman at the front of the room.

"Jan, I'd like you to meet my friend Rebecca. This is her first time, so be gentle. Okay?"

The three ladies laughed.

"Welcome," said Jan. "Don't worry, Rebecca. You're in safe hands. There is no judgement or expectation. Yoga unites the mind, body, spirit through breath and movement in harmony. You customize the poses for what your body will allow you to do. Do what you can in your own way without force. Take things slow and easy, especially at the beginning. I do hope you'll enjoy the practice and I know you'll benefit from the exercises."

"Thank you, Jan. Cissy says I need to learn how to breathe properly. I didn't know there was a right way or wrong way. I just figured breathing was automatic and have never given it much thought at all."

"Yes, most people don't," laughed Jan. "Well, let's get started."

Jan gently sounded a soft-toned gong and asked everyone to take their places on their mats.

Rebecca moved through all the postures gently as the teacher had suggested. Muscles that hadn't been used in a while groaned and she laughed at herself when she tried the 'Downward Dog'. After forty minutes the exercise portion of the evening was over and Jan instructed everyone to lie down on their mats and close their eyes.

"Oh,oh, here we go."

Jan turned down the lights and put a CD in the player. Turning it on, she spoke.

"As you all take a deep breath in through your nose, place your hands lightly on your belly...suspend the breath for a moment...slowly breathe out through your mouth. Another breath in...feel it travel in through your nose, throat, lungs, expanding your diaphragm...suspend the breath...and release through your mouth. Again, slow breath in...feel your belly rise...suspend...slow breath out...feel your belly fall."

As Jan was talking, she silently glided across the floor to where Rebecca was lying and covered her with a soft, warm blanket. Continuing to speak, she led the group into a visualization of being on a warm beach, easing them into the bliss of the vastness of the ocean...becoming one with it and all of nature...uniting.

Jan continued to talk and Rebecca felt her body sinking into a deep relaxation. Her shoulders dropped, it seemed for the first time ever, her jaw unlocked and opened. Her stomach softened and stilled like water on a smooth pond. Sinking deep into the moment, she completely surrendered, loose and reposed. Time had no meaning, no past, no future...just the now. Gradually, Rebecca became aware of Jan's voice calling them back to the room.

"Take your time coming back, bringing your awareness back into the room and into your body. I'll gradually turn the lights up. I would suggest you move slowly, keeping your peace as you roll up your mat and fold your blanket. Please eat something from the refreshment table to help ground yourself back into the present reality."

Rebecca sat up and looked around. The room came back to life bit by bit and people started chatting with each other.

"So, how was it for you?" asked Cissy, with a grin.

"Huh, oh, fine, fine. I'm not fully awake yet. Actually, it was amazing. I've never felt so relaxed in my life. Wow. There really isn't any woo woo stuff."

"Told you. Think you'd like to come again?"

"Yeah... I think I would. Let's go get something to eat. I'm starved."

"You're always starved," laughed Cissy. "But yeah, let's go. Gotta feed the physical as well as the spiritual."

That yoga class was the first of a number of 'woo woo' things that Rebecca had been introduced to by Cissy. She laughed at some of Cissy's weirder escapades; the trip to India to meet a world famous Guru; her studies with a Native American Shaman in Arizona; her trip to England to find a Celtic Witch and many more. Rebecca had always felt she was above such nonsense and had secretly been amused by Cissy's 'search' as she called it. Now Rebecca was glad she had someone to talk to who wouldn't think she was nuts. Despite their differences the two had grown very close throughout the years. They had shared many adventures together: the holidays to find fun and men; Cissy's rising prominence in her profession; Cissy's loss of her mother; the men in their lives; Rebecca finally finding David Connacher, 'the one'; their wedding; the birth of the twins...so many little day to day details of lives lived. Now, one more adventure to share and Rebecca wasn't at all convinced that she would be happy about where this one would lead.

Chapter Eleven

$\mathcal{D}$uring the long drive home images she had seen during the day replayed in her mind. The hallucinations, as she called them, had freaked her out at first, but now that she had time to think about it, she was convinced her mind was playing tricks on her. She drove through her gates and parked the car in front of the house. Entering the doorway, she called out. "I'm home."

Mrs. Brown came to the foyer from the back kitchen wiping her hands on her apron. She smiled. "Did you have a nice afternoon, Ms. Wainwright?"

"Yes, I had a lovely drive. Dr. Walsh will be here soon. Could you please bring us a cup of tea to the library? I'm just going upstairs to freshen up a bit and I'll be down in a few sec's."

"Oh, course. That will be no problem. The girls have gone over to your Mother's place for a visit, so I'll make sure that you are not disturbed."

"That would be lovely, thank you."

Rebecca climbed the stairs and went to the ensuite attached to her bedroom. After having a quick wash and a change of clothes, she descended the stairs and strode to the library. Booting up her computer, she entered all the information from the tombstone and Doris that she could remember into a Word document. Once her list was made she printed it out, so she could carry a hard copy with her. She then googled the information on the Realtor that held the listing for the cottage. Reviewing the information she noted that the house had been built sometime in the 1860's. That jibed with what Doris had told her. Mrs. Brown rapped on the door and opened it to let in Cissy and bring in the tea tray. Once Mrs. Brown had placed the tray on the coffee table, she left the room and closed the door, Cissy spoke.

"Okay, tell me what all the excitement is about and why you wanted me over here ASAP?"

"Man, what a story. I'm not sure I believe it and I was there! Let's get our cuppa and some of these cookies. I need the sustenance!"

Both ladies got their tea and then sat around the desk in the library.

"I don't even know how to begin," said Rebecca as she launched into her story.

"Damn. No wonder you panicked," said Cissy."

"Ya think? I've been going over and over everything that happened and I just can't get my head around it. Here's a list I printed out of what the caretaker told me about the place. I was just going to call the Realtor to see what he has to say. I need find out more about that house. Wanna help with the research to find out what's going on?"

"You bet. Oooooo, this is exciting. Our own ghost hunt."

"Ghosts? Bugger it. A hallucination that's all it was. My mind playing tricks on me."

Cissy sighed. "Get off it, girlfriend. We've been friends long enough now for you to have learned that there is more to life than just what you know with your five senses. Honestly, you can be so stubborn. Of course, they were real. It's not your meds and they're not hallucinations. Now you're part of your very own ghost story. How cool is that?"

"Not 'cool' at all. I don't want to be part of a ghost story. Crap. If the press ever found out... I can see the headlines now. Pampered daughter of the late Charles Wainwright gone completely off her rocker and seeing ghosts. The tabloids would have a field day. I'm sure Dr.

Holden will just love this little tidbit when I tell her. She'll be able to retire with what I pay her."

"Don't be ridiculous, Becca. If the ghost is stuck, maybe we'll be able to help her get to the light. That would be awesome."

Rebecca looked at Cissy as if she had two heads.

"Awesome? Not! I can do very well without this kind of awesome, thank you very much."

"What's the matter with you? You really piss me off sometimes! Why can't you accept what's in front of your face. Stubborn doesn't begin to describe you. Okay, have it your way. Let's at least see what you've written so far." Picking up the sheet that Rebecca had printed out, Cissy looked it over and said. "I know the area was settled in the 1830's and the Whitby Harbour was a port of entry for a lot of people. There were a ton of different kinds of mills, especially grist mills in that part of Ontario. In fact, Brooklin was a milling centre in the 1840's. Some of England's finest came out to Canada to build up their family businesses and mark their presence in the new world. I wonder if Mr. McBride had anything to do with the mills or their owners. Doris said he was a stone mason so maybe he worked on some of the larger estates in the area."

"How do you know that?"

"Oh, I was thinking of moving out there to join Lakeridge Hospital and did a little research on the background of the hospital as well as the region. The main library in Whitby has an archive section that deals with the settlement of this part of Ontario. I love doing research and visiting old cemeteries to get a feel for the terrain. It's fun."

"Only you would think it's fun to visit old cemeteries. Anyway, the library sounds like a good place to start. Do you have any free time in the next few days?"

"Actually, I do. I just finished a major project and had planned to take a few days off next week, so the timing is perfect."

"Don't miss your vacation on my account. I can go to the library alone and give you a call after."

"Not on your life. I was going to do a little redecorating. Blah. Colour swatches and paint chips. No thanks, I'd much rather join you. Just name the day and time and I'll be here."

"Thanks. I haven't told David anything yet as he'll think that I've completely lost it. I'd like to get some concrete answers before I bring it up. I'm drawn to that house so I want to know more about who lived there. Let's call the Realtor to see what he has to say."

Rebecca picked up the phone and dialed the number she'd written on the paper.

"Murray Addison," a voice on the other end of the phone answered.

"Mr. Addison, my name is Rebecca Wainwright and I am interested in a listing on your website. It is the house and grounds near Port Perry that was built around 1860."

"Yes, Ms. Wainwright. I know the place. How can I help you?"

"I would like to know about its history. What can you tell me?"

"Well, it was built by a Mr. William McBride who was an early settler to this part of the world. He named it Stone Cottage. From what I understand, he lived there with his wife and daughter until their untimely deaths in the 1870's. The property eventually went to William's brother and has been passed down through the family. The couple who currently own the land have been sub-letting it over the past few years. The last person who rented the house was an author trying to complete a novel. He required something a little out of the way and quiet, but he didn't stay too long. It's been vacant for the last couple of years, except for the housekeeper that comes in every couple of weeks to keep an eye on things. Any maintenance or upgrades have been looked after. The owners have moved to the States and are now anxious to sell. I could arrange for a viewing of the house if you wish."

"Thank you, Mr. Addison at the moment I am just gathering information. I was wondering if you knew where I could obtain more material about the original owners and their families."

"Well, I'm not sure what you could find out. Perhaps the Whitby library could be of assistance. I believe they have an archive of very old historical collections on the settling of the Durham community. Maybe they would have more details. Also, the land office might be able to tell you more about how Mr. McBride got the land. I'm sorry, but I don't know anything other than what I've told you. Are you interested in the property?"

"Yes, I am, but I want to do some research first. Here is my number. Please keep me informed of any offers you may receive. I will be in touch with you shortly to arrange a viewing. Thanks for your help."

"My pleasure, Ms. Wainwright. I will be sure to keep your number on hand and will give you a call if anyone else shows an interest. I look forward to speaking with you soon."

Rebecca hung up the phone.

Rubbing her hands together and licking her lips Cissy spoke. "He confirmed what the housekeeper said, so that's a good start. Open another Word document and we'll make a to-do list."

She and Rebecca worked for over an hour compiling a list of all of the details that they had heard about the property and adding what should be their 'next steps'. They retrieved the addresses and phone numbers of the Library and Land Registry Office from the web.

Rebecca called the Registry Office and the library to make appointments to visit. She and Cissy printed off the list and discussed how they planned to tackle the research.

"Well, I have to go sweetie, I've got that conference call."

"Okay, but you'll be back tomorrow?"

"Sure thing, wouldn't miss it for the world. Bye."

After Cissy left, Rebecca picked up her tea and wandered to her favourite spot in the sunroom. She lay down on her chaise and closed her eyes thinking about how her life had taken a bizarre twist. Two years ago she wasn't even thinking about a sanctuary of her own. She had the world by the tail. Now was a complete one eighty from then. Had it really been less than two years since the morning she had gone to the office for that board meeting with Chandler Industries, the pursuant argument with her Dad and the illuminating discussion with her brother?

Chapter Twelve

$\mathscr{R}$ebecca left her father's office. She paused for a moment at Janine's desk. Mustering her dignity, she drew herself up ramrod straight.

"No matter what my father says, I wish to be notified of any change, discussion, meeting or anything else to do with any of my projects. Is that perfectly clear?"

"Yes, Ms. Wainwright. I'll be sure to notify you from now on."

Rebecca continued on down the hall to her own suite of offices. Reaching her assistant's desk, she stopped for a moment.

"Mary, please hold all my calls for the next hour."

Mary looked up from her computer screen surprised. "You're back already? I thought the meeting would go at least another hour." Mary frowned as she studied Rebecca's face. "Are you okay? You don't look well, are you having another migraine? Oh, dear...did the Chandler's back out of the deal?"

"Yes, I am back, and no, the Chandler's didn't back out. You're right about the migraine though, so I just need quiet and solitude to get it under control. It's a long story. Everything is fine. Please bring me a cup of tea, some aspirin and the Davenport file."

"Yes, Ms. Wainwright, I'll get on it right away."

Rebecca watched Mary go to the small kitchen that was beside her office and then opened the door to her sanctuary. The muted tones, thick broadloom and darkness soothed her aching head. She quietly closed the door and crossed the room to a comfortable couch which beckoned to rest her weary body. She kicked off her shoes and sank down into its comfortable depths. Stretching out, she tried to let her mind go and think about nothing, as Cissy had taught her, but she had never quite been able to master the technique. Her mind was always racing trying to keep one step ahead of the competition while taking care of her family and keeping the home front in some sort of order. She thought about Cissy and smiled. Her best friend, sister from another mother. They had been through so much together and she loved her even more than she did her birth brother. Cissy gave her balance and helped to soften the hard edges she had been forced to adopt as a result of trying to compete in the world of corporate Canada. Wainwright Industries had been founded by her Great Great Grandfather as a small garment manufacturing business. It had grown into a worldwide conglomerate of fashion houses, textile mills...you name it...if it had anything to do with clothing of any sort, Wainwright Industries was probably involved somehow.

A small tap came from the door. It opened and Mary brought in a tea tray with a bottle of aspirin and a blue file folder. She set them down on the table in front of the couch.

Sitting up, Rebecca said, "Thank you, Mary. I really appreciate this. Do you have a lot on your plate for today?"

"I have the research I've gathered on the Montgomery acquisition to finish and then I need to review the work that Kyle has done for us regarding the Chandler account. Other than that, I can clear my desk. What can I do to help you?"

"No, Mary, I don't need you for anything else today. In fact, I'm in no mood to start something new so I'm going to putter around in here and call it an early night. We've been together...what...fifteen years?"

At Mary's nod, Rebecca smiled at her and continued.

"I am very grateful for the excellent work that you do and for your loyalty to me and the company. I want you to know how much I appreciate your patience and persistence. Please, take the rest of the day off. In fact, it's Thursday now. Why don't you clear both our calendars and we'll take an extra-long weekend. Lord knows we need it."

"Thank you, Ms. Wainwright. I appreciate your confidence in me. You've taught me so much about business from the time we started together, that I feel very fortunate to have this position. I will clear our calendars and leave as soon as I've finished. Have a great weekend. I hope your headache feels better soon."

"Thanks, Mary. Please close the door quietly on your way out."

Mary left the room, leaving Rebecca alone in the dark with her thoughts. She picked up the aspirin bottle and shook a couple out into her hand. After downing them with her tea, she lay back down on the couch and pulled an afghan over herself. A while later she stirred. What time was it? She looked at her watch, which read two o'clock. Well, at least her headache was better. Time to go home and have that long weekend with her family.

Cissy would be proud, she thought smiling. *She's always encouraging me to relax and 'get out into nature' as if that would solve all the problems of the world.*

She picked up her Michael Kors tote, grabbed her car keys and with one last look around her office, walked out to enjoy her mini holiday.

Chapter Thirteen

*R*efreshed from quality time with her family, Rebecca started the next week with vigour and a new outlook. No longer would she allow her father to push her buttons. She would show him instead that she was as capable as any man of running the company and had the numbers to prove it. Lost in her work, Rebecca looked up as she heard a knock on her door. Her brother poked his head into her office.

"May I come in?"

"Sure. What can I do for you?"

James walked into the room and sat in one of Rebecca's chairs. "First of all, I want to talk to you about last Thursday. I didn't know Pop hadn't talked to you before the meeting. I assumed you couldn't make it and were okay with me filling in. I don't know why he does that to you."

"Because I'm his 'little girl'. Add in the fact his conviction of who should be at the helm of a business empire is firmly entrenched in the male of the species, he'll always chose to have you in on any final consultations. But I've told him I'm going to bring him into the 21st century yet."

"Good luck with that. You're not the only one trying to bring the company forward. I've got some great ideas to get us out of the Stone Age, but he won't listen to any of them. He says the way the company is run was fine for his father and that's fine for him."

James stood and paced back and forth in front of Rebecca's desk swiping his fingers through his hair. Rebecca was taken aback. It had been a long time since she had seen her brother so agitated. Impeccably dressed in St.

Laurent, with his perfect grooming and style, he was always in complete control of himself, the epitome of today's metrosexual. He turned back to the desk and slumped in a chair. "Honestly, Bec, we really have to do something to make him see that Wainwright is becoming a dinosaur and will go extinct if we don't evolve. It's so frustrating. I think we should sell off some of the less profitable divisions and concentrate on our core business. Use some of the money from the sale to bolster R&D and bring in a new, fresh look to our boutiques. He won't listen. He puts me off when I suggest a discussion about updating the company. You've always been Pop's favourite. Shit. I've had to work twice as hard as you to get him to acknowledge that I know what I'm doing."

"Really? You're the heir apparent, not me. He'll never recognize what I accomplish because I'm a woman. It's humiliating. "

"Wow, I've always been jealous of your relationship with him. I thought you'd be the one sitting in the CEO's chair, not me. Don't you want it?"

"Apparently, not as much as you do. Funny, I never really believed that you cared about the company. I thought it was just a job to you and you'd probably sell if a profitable takeover bid was made."

"Sell? I don't want to sell. This corporation is our legacy. It's our family. I love this company. I'm hoping Benji will want to be a part of it when he gets older. I've always been proud to be a Wainwright and I've got some major proposals to put my own stamp on the business."

"Really? I had no idea you felt that way. I'm beginning to think we've been played. I'll bet he's pitted us against each other to make us fight for what we want. We should team up. If we approach him together he won't be able to sidestep around us so easily. Maybe we can get him to loosen his grip. It'll be interesting to see if we can get the mighty Charles Wainwright to bend."

Rebecca and James had their meeting with Charles and to say it was tumultuous was an understatement. Finally, after many negotiations, Charles agreed to allow James to implement some of his less, as he called them 'disruptive ideas'. Everything settled back to normal and Rebecca's life was once again perfect and in control.

Chapter Fourteen

*R*ebecca stood up from the chaise in the sunroom and started to pace. Everything had been so perfect. She and James were getting along better than they ever had. The business was going well and her new marketing strategies were about to be implemented. She was completely blindsided by what happened next. The date when her world collapsed was seared into her brain.

Friday, April 3rd began like any other day. Rebecca arrived at her office early and was seated at her desk, crunching some numbers when Mary buzzed through on the intercom. She frowned. "Mary, I said I didn't wish to be disturbed."

"I apologize, Ms. Wainwright, but Mr. Connacher's on the line. He says it's very important."

"Fine, put him through. David? What's going on?"

"It's Pop, he's had a heart attack. He's at Sunnybrook. I'm coming to pick you up. James is already there with your Mom."

Her heart cramped and she couldn't breathe. "W-w-what?" she stuttered.

"Pop and your brother had a meeting with the Anderson Group this morning. James stopped by the house to pick him up. When he got there, Mom told him Pop was in the greenhouse tending to his orchids. He went out to the small conservatory and there he was, puttering around. James called to him and as Pop turned, he crumpled to the ground. James rushed over, but he wasn't breathing. After calling 911 he started CPR. The paramedics came in a matter of minutes. They managed to bring Pop around and get him into the ambulance. After they left, James called me. He took your Mom to the hospital and I told him I would come and get you. I've left the girls with Mrs. Brown and I'm on my way."

"Get here as soon as you can. I'll be waiting." She hung up the phone. She hit the intercom button. "Mary, I need you."

Mary rushed into the office.

"My Dad's had a heart attack and David is on the way to pick me up as we speak. Please cancel all of my appointments for the rest of today. Do not let anyone else know of this just yet, I don't want to panic the shareholders. I'll call you with an update as soon as I know anything."

"Yes, Ms. Wainwright. I hope you'll find Mr. Wainwright feeling much better."

You and I both, thought Rebecca as she grabbed her tote and hurried out of the office. She arrived on the sidewalk just as David pulled up in front of her building.

"I've called James and told him we're on our way," said David as she climbed into the car. She nodded.

Please, hold on Daddy. You can't die. What would I do without you? Hang on, I'm coming.

Flying down the Don Valley Parkway, images of her father raced through Rebecca's mind. Pictures of him at home in his garden; on the boat at the cottage; playing catch with the children; presiding over a shareholders' meeting all ran together through her head. Anxiety made Rebecca's stomach hurt as if it had been pulled tight against her backbone. Arriving at the hospital she opened the door the car door, bolted from her seat and ran to the entrance. Her brother was standing just inside the doorway waiting for her. Throwing herself into his arms, she hugged him as hard as she could, tears streaming down her face.

"Where is he? Is he okay?" she asked.

"Yes, he's alive and resting. He's in intensive care...but you need to calm down a bit before you see Mom. She's pretty overwhelmed by the whole thing."

"Yes, yes, of course."

Closing her eyes, Rebecca took a deep breath to calm herself. She needed to focus. Every nerve ending was screaming to hurry, hurry. Her heart was racing. Finally, after several deep breaths, years of self-control conditioning kicked in and she stopped visibly shaking. She nodded to James, who took her arm and led her to the floor of the ICU. David parked the car and joined them. Rebecca approached the nurses' station outside the ICU and asked to see her father. The nurse checked with her supervisor and after receiving the okay, she unlocked the door and Rebecca pushed her way through. James and David went to the waiting room. Her Mom was seated in a chair by the side of one of the hospital beds. She was holding the hand of an elderly gentleman who was lying very still. Pop-pop? No, that shrunken old man was not her Dad. He couldn't be. This man was small and Pop-pop was huge. He was full of laughter and fun, not quiet and still like this poor person. His eyes were always twinkling with mischief, not closed and shuttered. Her steps faltered as she walked towards her mother. The sterile smell of antiseptic crept into her nostrils, finally registering in her brain. The whooshing sound of the machines, the static call over the loud speakers, "Dr. Humphreys, Dr. Humphreys, please report to the emergency room", buzzed in her ears. Bile rose up in her throat. Icy fear, like an arctic ice cap had melted on top of her head, cascaded down her body from head to foot. Taking the cold hand of the man in the bed, she whispered.

"Daddy, it's me, Becca. I'm here. Open your eyes and give me a smile."

Slowly, with great effort, the man on the bed opened his eyelids. "You're here", he sighed.

"Yes, I'm here, Daddy."

"Look after your Mother."

"Of course I will, Daddy."

"Just need to rest."

Rebecca watched as her father relaxed completely and fell into a deep sleep. She looked at her Mother. Isabella seemed to have aged ten years since yesterday. She resembled a wizened old crone, tears silently streaming down deep lines etched into her face and falling heedlessly into her lap.

"Oh, Momma," sobbed Becca, her hot tears falling onto her father's hand.

The door to the hospital room opened. David came over to the bed and put his hands on her shoulders. "C'mon sweetheart, he needs to rest. Let's see if we can find the doctor and get an update. Mom, we're just going out to the waiting room. Would you like to come with us, or would you rather stay here? Mom? "

Rebecca's mother's turned to David and gave him a sad smile. She spoke as if from a long distance away. "I'm sorry, David, did you say something?"

"Just that Rebecca and I are going to the waiting room to talk to James and the doctor. Would you like to come with us, or would you rather stay here?"

"I'll just wait here, if you don't mind. I don't want to leave him right now. You go along. Let me know what the doctor says, but I need to be here."

"Will do. Pop'll be fine, I'm sure."

David reached for Becca's hand to help her to her feet. They walked around the bed to her mother's side. Rebecca gave her mother a hug and kissed her cheek. Her Mother's skin was soft and fragile. It was like tissue paper that had been crumpled and smoothed out, leaving tiny crinkles that would never go away.

When did they grow old? How odd. I didn't notice.

She straightened her body and turned into David's arms as they walked out of the ICU and down the hall into a little waiting room. They found James, and his wife,

Katherine already there. David led Becca over to a chair beside James and eased her into it.

"I'll go find the Doctor," he said, as he turned and left the room.

"What happened? He was fine when I spoke to him yesterday. This can't be happening."

James replied, "He was fine, Bec. The paramedics said it was a good thing I was there and started CPR. They got him to the ICU, but he had another attack while they were getting him settled. They had to use the paddles to bring him back this time. He's hooked up to the machines and they are watching him. I don't know any more than that."

Just then, David came through the doorway with a young woman dressed in scrubs.

"Mr. Wainwright, Ms. Wainwright, I'm Dr. Samantha Choudry, your father's cardiologist. Mr. Wainwright Senior has had two heart attacks, but at the moment he is stable. The next forty-eight hours will be critical and we will be monitoring him closely. If he should respond to the treatment, we will move him to the cardiac floor within the next three days. If he continues to respond, he will be able to go home by next week."

"But how is he?" asked Becca. "Is he going to get better?"

"I don't know, Ms. Wainwright, we'll have to wait and see. As I said the next forty-eight hours will tell the story. You are welcome to stay, but there is really nothing that you can do for him tonight. He's resting comfortably right now. Why don't you take your Mother home? She's had a very long and trying day. We have your phone number and will call if anything further develops. I'm sorry, but I must go. It's been a very busy day."

Rebecca sat down on the chair nearest to where she had been standing. She covered her face with her hands. A shudder went through her body. She began to sob. This couldn't be happening! Not her father. Her anchor. Her rock. She was numb.

"He's going to die," she sobbed. "I just know he's not going to make it."

"Now, Becca," responded James. "You don't know that. The doctor said he has a good chance. Don't give up on him. Why don't you go home and get some rest? We'll take Mom with us for the night. Come to our place in the morning and we'll talk about what's next."

Chapter Fifteen

*T*he next several days were a blur for Rebecca. On Monday she went into the office, although she could not have told you what she did. At night, she stayed with her mother in the home where she had grown up. Monday evening, she went into the library, which smelled of lemon furniture polish, leather and her father's favourite Old Spice cologne. She wrapped herself in his sweater and curled up in his chair, weeping.

Isabella found her there. She went over to the chair and sat on the arm to stroke her daughter's hair. Rebecca looked at her mom and was immediately wrapped in her arms. For the first time in days, she felt the old sensation of comfort and safety. How many times had these arms held her just like this, when some drama in her life threatened to undo her? The nights when she'd cried herself to sleep because some boy had dumped her or the experiment with hair dye had turned her beautiful locks orange, instead of the 'radiant red' promised on the box. Now, the crisis was real but the arms about her still offered the same comfort as they had a million times before. Rebecca inhaled that comfort until she suddenly realized that her mother was not in her room sleeping, as she was supposed to be.

"Oh, Mom. I'm sorry. I didn't mean to disturb you. I came into the library because I feel his presence here and I can't bear to think of life without him."

"You didn't disturb me, sweetheart. I find it hard to sleep these nights without your Dad beside me so I was just coming down to fix a cup of hot chocolate when I heard a noise. I thought it might be you. The doctor phoned this morning to say he is improving and they will move him out of the ICU into a room this morning. We'll have him home by Friday if all goes well."

Rebecca felt an icy chill go up and down her spine but she couldn't tell her mother she wasn't at all sure about that.

"C'mon. Let's raid the kitchen and get that hot chocolate. I want to hear how the girls are doing at school. Didn't you say that Bella had soccer tryouts coming up?"

Together the two women strolled down the hallway to the warm kitchen trying to find a glimmer of happiness in what was a cloudy, unsettling picture of their future.

On Tuesday, April 7th, her father was moved to a bed in a private room at the hospital. Rebecca stopped by in the afternoon to visit him.

"Well, well, what's this," asked her father when she popped into his room. "Playing hooky are we?"

"What, the Executive VP of Wainwright Industries can't take a few moments for the important business of visiting the sick? If that's true, then I'd say we have to change our 'compassionate' policy, wouldn't you?" she laughed. "Especially when it's the Chairman of the Board I'm visiting."

Charles laughed with her. "It's good to see you, my dear. How are you doing? How are things at Wainwright?

"Everything's fine, Daddy. You are NOT to worry about the office. Do you understand me?"

"Aye, aye, Captain. I'll be good."

"You see that you are, or you'll answer to me!"

Rebecca sat on the edge of her father's bed and held his hand in hers. His warmth and strength seeped into her very bones and she relaxed a little for the first time since she had learned of his heart attack. Smiling at him, she saw the twinkle come into his eyes as he gazed back at her. They sat for a few moments, quietly content to be in one another's presence. No words were needed.

"I'm so proud of you, my sweet. You have made me a very happy man. Of course, I adore your mother and am thrilled with James, but you and I have always had something special, haven't we? Now, I need you to do something very important for me. I've realized over the past few days that I will not always be around. Your mother will need you more than ever if I go. So, I need you to promise me that you will look after her."

"Oh, Daddy," Rebecca squeezed his hands a little tighter. "Don't talk like that. You are getting better and will be home next week. But if it makes you feel easier, then I promise."

Charles patted her hand. "There's a good girl. I don't anticipate leaving anytime soon, but I want to you to know what I need, just in case. Now, let's talk about those granddaughters of mine. Is Amy going to be in the spring play? Tell her to 'break a leg' for me. She'll be a knockout. I think we have a budding star on our hands."

Rebecca began to tell him all about her daughters' escapades and they spent a wonderful hour together. "Well, I'd better get back to work or the boss might fire me and you need to get some rest. Please take care of yourself, Daddy. I need you back home again."

Smiling, she leaned down to give her father a kiss. Sitting back, she gently traced the outline of his face with her fingers and then reached around to give him an extra hug. She felt those strong arms hug her back. As long as she had those arms, she would never feel frightened. They had been a source of safety and support her whole life. With her father near, she felt invincible. She took a moment now to absorb into her very core the feeling of love and security that they gave to her.

"Bye, Daddy. You have a good sleep and we'll see you tomorrow."

"Goodbye, my love. I'll see you later."

Rebecca gave her dad's hand one last squeeze and walked to the door. In the doorway she turned and blew him a kiss. As Charles raised his hand in farewell and returned her kiss, Rebecca left the room.

Chapter Sixteen

*R*ebecca remembered how David had shuffled his schedule so that during the day he was able to drive Rebecca's mom back and forth to the hospital to visit her husband. She picked up the photo album that was lying on the table beside the chaise. She opened it and looked at the pictures of her father that were there. She stroked the images gently letting her tears fall onto the page. She read again the death notice that had been put into the newspaper.

"Oh, Daddy, I miss you so much."

Her hand lingered on her favourite photograph of her Dad and her at the annual summer picnic the year before he died. Such happy times. Then she thought about the worst day of her life. The day that she would never forget for as long as she lived. The one when her perfect life exploded into tiny fragments she would never be able to repair.

***

On Wednesday, April 8th, Rebecca was sitting in her office when the phone rang.

"Rebecca Wainwright."

"Becca, it's David."

"You're calling early today. What's up? Are Mom and Dad having a little gossip session and you're feeling left out?" She smiled into the phone thinking of the little tete-a-tetes that her parents had been sharing, and how David felt a little awkward around them as if he were intruding on very private space.

"Sweetheart, Pop passed away about an hour ago. I'm coming to get you."

Rebecca's heart shattered into a million pieces. Her whole body shook with the force of the destruction. Her mind tried to grasp what David had said. It couldn't be right. Pop was coming home this week. David must be joking, but he would never joke about a thing like this.

"What? No, no!" she screamed. "That can't be right. No!"

Hearing Rebecca's scream, Mary came running into the office. "Ms. Wainwright," she cried. "What's happened, are you all right?"

Rebecca slumped in her chair, the phone still clasped in her hand. "Becca, Becca," it said.

Hearing the voice, Mary picked up the phone. "This is Ms. Wainwright's Assistant, Mary. I'm sorry, but she's unable to come to the phone at the moment. May I assist you?"

"Mary, this is David. Mr. Wainwright Senior passed away this morning and I've just told Rebecca. I am on my way to the office to pick her up. Will you please stay with her until I get there?"

"Oh, no. Of course I will. I'll attend to everything, Mr. Connacher." Mary hung up the phone and quickly brought Rebecca a shot of brandy from the sideboard in the office. "Here, drink this. Your husband will be here soon. Don't you worry about a thing. I'll cancel all of your appointments and meetings. Why don't you come over to the couch and lie down until Mr. Connacher gets here?"

"No, I must call Cissy. I need her."

"That's fine,. Why don't I get her on the phone while you drink the brandy? It will help."

Mary picked up the phone and quickly dialed the number. "Dr. Walsh, this is Mary from Rebecca Wainwright's office. I'm sorry to disturb you but she needs you. She has just received word that her father passed away this morning."

"Oh, no," replied Cissy. "Is she all right? I thought he was getting better. Put her on the phone...no, wait. Tell her that I'll be there ASAP. Is David with her? Oh, my poor Becca."

"She's not doing very well, Dr. Walsh. I don't know all of the details, but Mr. Connacher was with him when he died and he's on his way to pick her up now. I'll tell her you're on your way."

Mary hung up the phone and put her arms around Rebecca. "C'mon, Ms. Wainwright. Let's get you over to the couch. Dr. Walsh is on her way." Mary led Rebecca to the couch and covered her with a blanket. She then dimmed the lights and quietly left the room.

Tears flowed freely from Rebecca's eyes and her body started to shake. She was so cold. She thought she might never be warm again. Her father was gone. That couldn't be right, there must be some mistake. She had seen him yesterday and told him she would be back today. How would she live without her Dad? She could see him now, standing in his greenhouse, tending his precious orchids. Those damn flowers! He loved them above anything else he owned. This is where she'd find him, when she went home. He had to be there, he couldn't be gone. She sat up and started to keen. Rocking back and forth, she couldn't stop the sobs that came from deep within her soul. She stared into the abyss of the years ahead without the love, guidance and strong arm of her father beside her. Thank God Cissy was on her way. She would know what to do.

Chapter Seventeen

*R*ebecca remembered when Cissy arrived at the office. Strong arms had encircled her. Becca clung to the embrace while sobbing out her heartache and grief. Making soothing noises and rubbing her back, Cissy held her friend as her own heart cracked at Becca's sorrow. After a while, her sobs subsiding, Becca leaned back against the sofa and shut her eyes.

"Oh, Cissy, I'm so glad you're here."

"Sweetheart, what happened? I thought he was getting better?"

"He was. David called and told me that he and Mother were sitting together over by the window. They were talking when he just leaned back in his chair and was gone. It was a massive heart attack and there was nothing anyone could do. But, that can't be right, can it? He can't be gone. He'll be home by the end of the week. That's what the doctor said. Yes, David made a mistake. You'll see. He was just resting for a moment in his chair. He gets quite tired since his first heart attack and I'm sure he was just resting. Oh, Cissy, what will I do without him?" Fresh tears spilled from her eyes and Becca turned an anguished face to her friend.

Rubbing Becca's hands, Cissy replied. "David and I will be right here with you. You do not have to do this alone. We'll just go one step at a time."

David entered the office. Rebecca looked up at him, her grief stricken eyes showing the pain and loss that radiated through her body. She leapt up and ran to him. He gathered her into his arms, surrounding her with all the love and comfort that had sustained them through the years.

Walking her over to the couch and sitting her down, he said.

"I'm so sorry it took me so long to get here. The hospital called James. I waited until he arrived so that he could stay with Mom while I came to get you. Mary is bringing us a cup of tea and we'll just catch our breath here for a few moments, before we head out to the hospital."

Mary brought in the tea service and placed it on the coffee table. David poured Becca a cup of strong, sweet tea and lifted the cup to her lips. As if in a trance, she slowly sipped the warm beverage. As the initial shock began to wear off some colour seeped into her face and her body gradually stopped shaking as warmth spread through her limbs. She took several deep breaths and felt calmer. She looked at David and found her strength returning under his compassionate gaze. Putting down the cup and saucer, David took her hands and gave them a squeeze.

"He's really gone? This is not a joke?" she said her eyes pleading with him to tell her it was all a mistake.

Stroking the back of her hands gently, David replied, "No, Sweetheart. It's not a joke or a mistake, he really is gone."

Rebecca lowered her eyes and took a big sigh. "Okay, I'm ready to go now."

"All right, we'll take it slowly."

The trio stood and walked out of the room. Mary was at her desk and, as they passed, David turned to her.

"Mary?"

"It's okay, Mr. Connacher. I've taken care of everything. I have cleared Ms. Wainwright's schedule for the next few weeks. I have notified the legal department and a press release will be in the evening papers. I have called the funeral home to let them know and I have notified Mr. Wainwright's lawyers about the situation. I'm so sorry, we had such high hopes that he was getting better.

If there is anything, anything at all that Ms. Wainwright needs, please let me know."

"Thank you. I don't know what we'd do without you. You are a Godsend. I'll keep in touch and let you know what's happening. Please, when you're finished, take the rest of the day off. The office will be closing for a few days anyway until we know what we'll be doing."

* * *

After escorting Rebecca to the car and settling her in, David pulled out of the parking lot and drove down the street with Cissy following. At the hospital, the three of them made their way to the small waiting room on the floor where her father's room was. James, Kat and her mother were already there.

"Oh, Mom," she cried rushing into her mother's arms where the two women embraced.

"Hush, hush. It's okay sweetheart," replied her mother, stroking Becca's head as she did when she was a small child.

"May I see him?"

"Of course. He's in the room."

"Cissy, will you come with me?"

"Certainly."

Lifting up her chin and straightening her shoulders, Rebecca walked out of the waiting room and down the hall to her Dad's room. Entering the room, she saw her father's body, lying on the bed. His eyes closed, he almost looked like he was asleep, but Becca knew that her father's life force was gone as the room felt cold and empty. The only noise she could hear was the traffic on the street below his window. She wished his eyes would open just once more to twinkle with love and laughter, but that was never going to happen. Only the shell of his body remained. Charles Wainwright, loving father and grandfather, confidante, businessman, pillar of the community, had crossed to another place and she could not follow.

She bent and kissed his brow.

"Goodbye, Daddy. Safe journey."

She took Cissy's arm and together they walked out of the room, leaving behind her perfect life.

Chapter Eighteen

*H*er mind went back to the days after his death, which had gone by in a blur. The notice was released to the paper, funeral arrangements finalized, flowers ordered, condolences received; all things to do with the closing of a life were complete. Rebecca had not been truly aware of any of it. A dark cloud swirled around her shielding her from everything and everyone. She was on autopilot. David and Cissy assisted her into the funeral parlour, but she didn't remember anything about the service. She accepted the condolences of friends and colleagues and attended the light supper supplied after the service, but she couldn't have told you who was there or what was served.

Arriving home, she went up to the bedroom, closed the curtains, stripped - leaving her clothes in a puddle on the floor - and climbed into bed. Contemplating life without her father was unbearable. Her mind shut down. All she wanted to do was go to sleep and never wake up.

The morning after the funeral, David entered the bedroom and kissed Rebecca's cheek. "Becca, sweetheart, time to get up."

"Don't wanna."

"Honey, please, wake up for me."

"No."

"Becca, please. Just for a little while."

"Tired, go 'way. Wanna sleep."

David left the room with a sigh. He watched his wife fall into a vortex of depression that spiralled deeper each day. Each morning as he entered their bedroom, he hoped she would get out of bed under her own steam, but that didn't happen. He spoon-fed her soup and tea, and attempted to coax her out of bed. Half carrying her to the bathroom, he attempted to give her a sponge bath. As well as caring for his wife, David called the doctor, fielded calls from work and friends, played both Mother and Father to their children and ran his business.

One day while fixing breakfast for the girls, he let out a howl of despair and swept his arm across the table. All of the dishes, utensils and food splintered in a thousand directions onto the floor. Feelings of rage, hopelessness and impotence mixed together in a toxic brew that pulsated through his body. He wondered if he would ever be able to piece it back together. He fell into his usual chair and put his face in his hands, huge sobs racking his body. "Becca, please, come back to me."

Out of the corner of his eye, he saw motion in the doorway. He lifted his head as his daughter raced to his side. She threw her arms around his neck and said, "Daddy, please don't cry. It'll be all right. Bella and I will be very good. We'll be very quiet and make her a pretty picture. That will make her happy. She's going to be better soon, I just know it. Please don't be upset."

Struggling to gain his composure, David straightened his shoulders and cleared his throat. Taking his daughter's hands he looked at her troubled young face. "Oh, Amy," he said. "I'm sorry if I scared you. This is not your fault. You and Bella have been very good. Mommy is upset that Pop-Pop has died, but you're right. She's going to be fine. Run along now, sweetheart. See if you can find Bella and Mrs. Brown, there's a good girl."

Tears glistened on Amy's eyelids. With a deep sigh, her head hanging down, she shuffled out of the kitchen.

David sat for a few minutes and then wearily reached for the phone. "Cissy," he said. "I'm at my wit's end. She's not any better. It's been almost two weeks since the funeral. The curtains are drawn in our room and she won't leave the bed. I've been sleeping in the guest room. I've managed to get a bit of soup down her, but she's just withering away. This morning I've had a meltdown in front of Amy and she's left the kitchen crying. The girls are scared she's going to die as well as Pop-Pop. Nothing I say reassures them."

"I'll be right there."

* * *

Cissy climbed the staircase and entered Rebecca's room. It smelled of stale air and rancid body odour. She opened the drapes and the windows to let in the sunlight and fresh air before she walked over and sat on the bed. Picking up Rebecca's hand, she said, "Hey, kiddo, time to wake up."

"Don' wanna. Bright. Too bright. Close the drapes."

"No, I will *not* close the drapes. This has gone on long enough. You need to get up, dressed and have something to eat. I'll be right here, but you need to do this. If not for yourself, for your husband and two beautiful daughters. They're missing their mother."

"I can't Cissy."

"Yes, you can, sweetheart and I'm going to help. First of all, I want you to sit up and swing your legs over the side of the bed."

Cissy put her arms around Becca's shoulders and helped her gently into a sitting position. She was able to feel the bones beneath her skin. Becca had always been slender, but this was alarming. "That's it. Now we're going to stand and walk to the bathroom."

Cissy put her arms around Rebecca's waist and helped her stand. Rebecca crumpled. Her legs were prickling and as the fog cleared from her mind, she realized she couldn't stand on her own. Her body tingled from

~ 99 ~

building anxiety. The air in her nostrils was icy cold as she breathed in a fast, shallow rhythm.

"Cissy, what's happening to me? Why can't I stand up?"

"You've been laying in that bed for over a week, so your leg muscles are beginning to atrophy. We'll just stand here until you get your balance before we move to the bathroom."

"It can't be that long. I know David has come to help me to the bathroom and bring me food, but I thought it was only a day or two at the most. I guess I've lost track of time."

"Well, it has been so you need to take things easy. C'mon, let's get you into the shower."

The two friends shuffled across the room and into the bathroom.

"Here, give me your nightgown. You get washed while I strip the bed. Call me when you're ready, and I'll help you dress."

Cissy turned on the shower and left the bathroom. Becca was dizzy as she climbed in and leaned against the wall for support. The warm water felt good on her body and she closed her eyes and let the mist of the shower spray flush away the cobwebs in her brain. Squeezing her favourite bath gel onto a soft sponge, she caressed her body in small circles, smelling the fragrance of the woody musk and reawakening her olfactory senses. She shampooed her hair letting all the grime, fetor and lethargy of the last week flow down the drain. Her senses awakened, and feeling human again, she turned off the water, stepped out of the shower and dried herself. Looking into the mirror, a stranger's reflection stared back at her.

Who's that scraggly old woman? Good heavens! That can't be me, can it?

Startled, feelings of guilt caused a flush to infuse her face.

C'mon, girl. You need to get your act together. Wainwright's do not give in to self pity. Get your butt in gear.

Stroking her skin with her favourite body butter reinvigorated her determination. Leaving the bathroom, she walked over to Cissy and gave her a hug.

"Thanks for coming to my rescue."

"Oh, honey, I couldn't let you wallow any longer. You know how much I love you but it was time for your Dad to move on to his next journey. We just have to figure out how we're going to deal with it."

An arrow of despair pierced Rebecca's heart. "I hear you, but I don't believe it was his time. He was still young. He and Mom had a whole bunch of things planned in the next few years. Why did God do this to me? It's not fair. I need him."

"I don't know why, Becca, but I know you're not going to get any answers holed up in this room. Let's get you dressed. We'll go downstairs and get something to eat. If you'd like, we can sit in the sunroom for a while, but I don't want you coming back up here until bedtime."

Together, the women descended the stairs and made themselves comfortable in the solarium. Rebecca nibbled on the small sandwiches, cheese and pastries that Mrs. Brown had provided. Setting her plate on the coffee table, she leaned back and closed her eyes.

"You know, I have listened to you all these years talk about a loving Universe and kind Creator, how we're all connected and other New Age mumbo jumbo. I've never really bought into what you believe. Now that my father has died, it really seems ludicrous. How could a loving God take away my father when I need him so badly? Your philosophy just doesn't make sense."

Cissy said nothing for a moment, gathering her thoughts.

"I'm sorry you think what I've shared with you over the years is all so much airy, fairy stuff. It's so much more than that. God didn't cause your father to die to hurt you. I believe before we come to this planet, we along with our soul group and Spirit Guides make a plan together - sort of like a blueprint for our life of what we want to accomplish while we're here. From what I've read there are different paths built into the plan depending on what we choose when we get here, including when to be born and when to go Home again. Your Dad completed what he wanted to do and simply went Home. We're all connected and though you can't see him, the two of you are still joined. I'm sure he'll make his presence known to you somehow. I don't know when or how, but you'll know it when it happens."

"Are you nuts? That's bizarre. Dad would never plan to leave me all alone. Choosing when we are born or when we die? It's a load of crap. You don't really believe that do you? I think you've been taken in by some fast talking snake oil salesman."

"Really? You think I'm that stupid?"

"No, you're kind and loving but not very practical - a perfect target for sleazebags."

"I can assure you I'm not that easy to con. Anyway, I came to help you get on your feet and out of bed. Mission accomplished. Get up each day and face yourself in the mirror. The girls are scared sick you're going to die. Show them you're still very much alive and kicking."

"Don't tell me what I need to do for my girls. They're MY children. You have no idea what it's like. I don't care about anything. A trip to Paris or a Caribbean cruise? Winning the lottery? Ha. A few months ago I would have loved any of those things. Now...I'm not interested. Nothing matters. There's a darkness so deep inside, I feel like I'm drowning in pain. He was my anchor, my rock. Who do I lean on now?"

"You and your Guides. You'll have to learn to trust your own guidance."

Becca jumped up from the chaise lounge. "I CAN'T DO THAT!" she screamed. "Haven't you heard me? What part of 'I need my Dad' don't you understand? I want him back. I want my life back."

"Okay, time for me to go. I'll return as soon as I can. Take care of yourself, honey. We'll talk soon."

As Cissy started to rise from her chair, Rebecca grabbed her hand. "Don't go. Please don't go. I'm sorry. I'm such an ass. I know you're only trying to help, but I'm not sure I can be helped. I never imagined a future without my Dad in it. I had everything...the perfect life, job, family... Now it's gone and I don't know what to do."

Cissy sat back down. Taking Rebecca's hands and looking her in the eye, she said. "I know, Sweetie. The centre of your universe has shifted and you're floundering. You can work through this. You don't have to have answers today - tomorrow or even next week. I love you, sister. We'll get through this together."

Chapter Nineteen

*R*ebecca remembered what it was like that first few months after the funeral.

I was so lost, but I had to keep up pretenses for David and the kids. It felt like I was climbing Mount Everest just to get out of bed every morning, but I did it. I got up, washed, dressed and put on my makeup. Major accomplishment! I was sure I could put on a good show and no one would ever know how much I was hurting. Ha. Little did I know...

***

A month after the funeral Rebecca returned to work and tried to function. She began to devise little rituals to calm herself down, before leaving the house. One habit she developed was glancing into the hall mirror above the tray that held her car keys, to see if the visage that looked back at her showed any signs of coming to life. Every day the face had the same dead eyes filled with dull despair. Each time there was no sign of improvement, Rebecca would sigh and wearily head out to the office to attend meetings; discuss business with Mary and sign papers, all done by rote. Devoid of feeling. At night she would crawl into bed exhausted. She couldn't even cry anymore. This routine continued for several months.

Rebecca remembered clearly that day in mid-July. She had been seated at her desk. Her mind on a file she wished to discuss with Mary, she got up and started walking to the door. As she rounded the corner of her desk, she experienced an intense sensation of vertigo. The world tilted on its axis and she stumbled into the table. Her heart rate accelerated. Waves of unfamiliar sensation undulated over her body. Terror pulsated through her mind, freezing her to the spot. Breathing became shallow and cold while dizziness so overwhelmed her she couldn't figure out which way was up and which was down. A loud buzzing started in her ears and her mouth became so dry her tongue stuck to its roof. The disequilibrium made her feel nauseous while her body wouldn't stop shaking. Heat surged in her torso until she felt like she would explode into a million pieces. Her very soul felt as if it were leaving her body. Heart attack! She was going to die. She tried to call out to Mary but no sound could come out of her mouth. She groped her way back around the desk and fell into her chair. With her eyes still closed she reached out and managed to press the intercom button.

"Yes, Ms. Wainwright?"

"Mary…" she managed to croak.

Within seconds the door opened and Rebecca heard Mary rush into the room.

"What's happened? Are you okay?"

"Don't know," said Rebecca stumbling over her words. She knew what she wanted to say, but her thoughts were disconnected from her speech centre and she couldn't enunciate them. "Feel terrible. Water…want water."

"Yes, of course. Sit there and I'll get you some."

A glass was placed in her hands and Rebecca downed the water.

"What happened? How can I help?"

Rebecca sat with her eyes closed trying to calm her racing heart. "Don't know. Be all right in a minute. Stay with me."

Mary pulled up a chair and gently rubbed one of Rebecca's hands. It was cold and clammy. After what seemed like an eternity, Rebecca's heart started to beat normally and the excessive heat died down. The dizziness decreased and the world righted itself. Her body stopped shaking and only the ringing in her ears remained. Opening her eyes she looked at her assistant.

"Mary, I don't know what just happened. I've never experienced anything like that before. Did I have a heart attack?"

"I don't know Ms. Wainwright. Let me call Mr. Connacher."

"Yes, please. I'm very tired and still shaky. I need David. He'll take me home."

Mary left the office to call David from her phone. Within a half an hour, David was at her side. "What happened, Sweetheart?"

Rebecca told him what she had experienced. "I'm just so tired now. Please take me home."

"Of course. First I want to get you checked out in case it was a heart attack. I called the doctor's office on my way here and she would like to see you right away."

"Okay."

David bundled Rebecca up and helped her out of the office and into the car. Arriving at the doctor's office, they were hustled into her examining room immediately. After an ECG and a few other tests, she faced David and Rebecca in her office.

"The good news is that it doesn't look like anything serious, but I can't be positive until I get the blood work and other tests back. What I suspect is that you've had a severe panic attack. I suggest bed rest for a few days. I will give you something so that you can sleep and relax. We will do a follow up appointment after that."

"A panic attack? What are they?"

"There really is no one known cause, but they can be associated with severe depression and/or stress. They can also be inherited. They usually happen without warning while you are doing ordinary activities. This may be a onetime thing, but I would advise you to ease up on your schedule and rest as much as you can. I'd like to see you again next week for follow up and we can discuss what treatments you will need, if any, from there. You may need to take a leave of absence for a few months to get this under control."

"A Leave of Absence? No can do. With my father's death, the office needs all hands on deck. I can't shirk my responsibility because my emotions have gotten a little out of control."

"Well, if you don't slow down, things could get much worse. Developing a debilitating panic disorder or agoraphobia isn't an impossibility."

Rebecca looked at David and reached out for his hand.

"Thank you for your advice, Doctor. Rebecca and I will continue this discussion at home, but we will come and see you next week.

* * *

Arriving home she told David she was going up to the bedroom to lie down for a while.

"All right, Becca, but I want to discuss this when you wake up. Why don't you take a nice long bath before you rest? It will help relax you. Just call when you are ready to come down and I'll fix us something to eat, while we talk about what happened and where we go from here."

"Okay, David. Just give me a couple of hours to sleep and then we'll talk."

Rebecca climbed the stairs to the bedroom. Once there she stripped down and slid into a warm bath to soothe her aching body and mind. The aroma of the lavender bath salts tickled her nose. She slithered down under the water and let her mind go blank. Her body relished the warmth and buoyancy of the water. She emptied her mind and drifted until the water began to grow cold. Reluctantly bringing herself back to reality, she pushed herself out of the tub and dried off. Wrapping her body in a soft bathrobe, she walked out into the bedroom and curled up in her reading chair. Thinking about the incident, heat rushed to her cheeks and she felt embarrassed by everything that had happened.

Well, that can't happen again. I'm not going allow a stupid panic attack get the better of me. I've always been in control. I will not let panic dictate who I am. I won't. I am not weak, I'm strong. I am Rebecca Wainwright, dammit.

She would listen to the doctor and lessen the stress in her life, but she was not going to take a leave of absence. James was relying on her help. She would talk to David, but nothing would make her give up her work. With a firm resolution in her mind, she closed her eyes and fell into a troubled sleep.

Even with all the determination in the world, Rebecca was helpless in the face of something she couldn't control or understand. Little by little, activities which were normal and fun began a slow deterioration. The cacophony of downtown Toronto which used to make her feel happy and energized, now rattled her. Walking on the street, terror would suddenly overwhelm making her feel as if the baying hounds of hell were on her heels and she needed desperately to run. She would look around to see what had prompted the sensation but everything was normal. Driving was daunting and she could no longer manage it. Travel by GO train or subway was out of the question. The thought that she might lose control sent her into frenzy. Crowds were impossible to navigate without suffering an attack so weekly dates with David at their favourite restaurant or theatre, ceased. In early September, she took a leave of absence from the office. Her home became her refuge. A whole day without panic was cause for celebration. Darkness clouded her mind and nothing brought a smile to her face. Her only focus was preventing another attack. Sorrow and despair were her constant companions and sometimes she felt that death would be a welcome release. Agoraphobia was a constant, safe companion.

Chapter Twenty

$\mathcal{C}$issy's heart ached as she watched her once vibrant, confident friend become a facade of her former self. Yes, Rebecca washed, dressed and puttered around the house, but her eyes were haunted and dull. She hadn't heard her laugh in months. Rebecca's heart was encased in a brittle shell effectively surrounding her with a protective shield which kept everyone at a distance. Cissy felt that shell would someday explode into a thousand pieces that no one would be able to put together again. She sought out David in his office.

"Hi. Can I come in?"

"Of course. What can I do for you?"

"I'm really concerned about Becca, she's getting so much worse. What can we do?"

"I don't know. Nothing interests her anymore and she's so afraid. I've suggested we go out for supper, or to the theatre, but she always begs off. These attacks she's been having, they're getting worse and now she won't leave the house at all. Even at home, she has several a day. Sometimes she wakes up in a full blown attack and it takes her a couple of hours to shower and dress. I got a reference for a Dr. Phyllis Holden, who's supposed to be excellent working with people who suffer from anxiety disorders. I called her office and an opening has come up, so I've booked it. I just hope she'll go."

"That's fabulous, David. We have to make her go. I can't stand to see her slipping away from us like this. Let me know how it goes."

Cissy left the house and David went in search of Rebecca. He found her out in the garden sitting in one of the lounge chairs. He approached her and bent down to give her a kiss on the forehead. Pulling a chair around to face her, he sat down. He picked up her hands and smiled.

"Hi, sweetheart. How are you feeling today?"

Rebecca smiled back. She loved this man with all her heart and felt guilty for all she was putting him through.

"I'm fine. I haven't had an attack in...let's see, what time is it? One o'clock? Wow, it's been four hours. That must be a record."

She looked at David, smiling while her eyes brimmed with tears. The two lovers gazed at each other for several moments. David's heart broke as he watched his beautiful wife shatter in front of him. Becca's sobs began low in her throat and the tears became an overflowing reservoir of pain and remorse.

"Oh, David, what is happening to me? I should be over my grief by now. What you must think of me. I'm such a mess," she sobbed clutching his arms.

David picked her up and settled her in his lap. Holding her tight while she cried, he stroked her hair and spoke soothing endearments to her. When she stopped and was quiet, he gently laid her back on her chaise. Still holding her hands, he spoke ever so softly to her.

"Becca, I want you to listen carefully to me. You're my wife and I love you. I'll never leave you. You are my heart and soul. You're ill at the moment. We are going to get through this together, but I need you to do something for me. I really think that you should see someone, professionally, who can help you get a handle on things. I've made an appointment with a Dr. Holden. Will you go see her?"

Rebecca wrapped her arms around herself in a rigid pose. She frowned and her eyes were like ice when she looked at her husband.

"She's a shrink, isn't she? You think I'm crazy, don't you? Is that why you want me to see her? I'm not crazy," she lashed out.

"No, I don't think you're crazy, but I do think you need a little help to get back on track. Just try it. If it doesn't work, we'll figure out something else. You don't have to keep going if you don't like her or what she is suggesting you do, but, for my sake and the girls, please try."

"You're ashamed of me, aren't you?"

"No, I'm not ashamed of you. I love you and I want you to get better. I want my wife back and the girls need their Mother."

"But, what if I can't get better, David. What if this is going to be who I am from now on? What then?"

"We'll deal with that if it happens, but for now, I just want you to try. Please."

Becca shut her eyes and lay back on the lounge.

"All right. For your sake and the girls, I'll go. I want to get better, but what if I can't. I'm scared, David. Why did this happen?"

"Sweetheart, you've had a lot on your plate this last year or so. The shock of Pop's death, pushing yourself at work, your charitable functions, coordinating the girls, and running the household, it's been too much and you've shattered. You've done nothing wrong. You will get better. It may take a while, but we are all here for you. James is fine at the office and Mary is looking after things for you while you're away. Just take this chance to start to heal. Please."

"All right. I'm so sorry that I've let you and everyone down. I never dreamed I could be like this. I've always felt people with emotional problems should just suck it up and get on with their life. It never dawned on me that it's not always possible."

"No one really understands what another person is going through, until it happens to them. You've not let anybody down. We'll get some help. Just try, that's all anyone can ask."

David sat with Becca holding her hand for a while until she fell asleep. He watched his wife and wondered at the strange turn their lives had taken. What would happen to her? What would happen to him and their family? He sure hoped that Dr. Holden had some answers. Little did he know from where the answers would come and how their lives would be changed.

Chapter Twenty-One

On the day of her first appointment with Dr. Holden, David was waiting for her at the bottom of the stairs.

"You look beautiful, darling. It's a lovely day and we're just going for a ride to meet Dr. Holden. I will be with you the whole time, so there's nothing to worry about."

Rebecca looked at her husband. Her heart squeezed and pain spread throughout her body. He was her everything but there was no words to explain how scared she was. An attack was always lurking around waiting to pounce. What if one happened while she was out? Other people would see and pity her. That couldn't happen. Straightening her spine, she stepped out of the front door and into the blinding sunlight. Overwhelming terror slammed into her. Rebecca stumbled over to the wall of the house and clung on, her breath coming in fast gulps. David had walked on to the car and didn't notice that she wasn't with him. He turned and saw her clutching the wall by the door. Quickly, he hurried back to her side.

"Becca, sweetheart, what's wrong?"

"Hold me, David. Just hold me. I'll be all right." She burst into tears. "Don't make me go, I don't want to. Please, David."

"It's okay, Becca. We'll walk down to the car. I'll be right here beside you."

David led her down to the car and helped her get in. Becca leaned her head back onto the seat and closed her eyes.

Please let the doctor be able to help.

On September fourteenth, five months after she had buried her father, Rebecca arrived at the Psychiatrist's office. She and David were led into a cheerful waiting room. Bathed in a soft blue with comfortable chairs, it looked less like a doctor's office and more like a sunny sitting room. Within a few moments, the doctor's receptionist called her name.

"Ms. Wainwright, Dr. Holden will see you now."

Rebecca's mouth went dry and tiny shivers of fear ran through her body. She lifted her chin, straightened her spine and walked resolutely into the office.

Dr. Holden looked to be in her mid-fifties, with a touch of gray at her temples and a few streaks of white in hair that was the colour of brown sugar. She had a round face with lively blue eyes that crinkled at the corners when she smiled. She was dressed in a lovely lavender blouse with a matching pleated skirt that swished like a kilt as she walked toward Rebecca.

"How do you do, Ms. Wainwright? Please come in and sit down. Can I get you something to drink? Water, perhaps?"

"No, thank you doctor. I'm fine."

"Good, then let's get started shall we? Please tell me what brings you to see me today."

Rebecca told her about her life and the recent events that had led her to Dr. Holden's doorstep.

"I don't understand what's happening. I've never thought of myself as weak before. I would have been the first one to say 'suck it up, sister' to anyone else in my position. I never dreamed I'd be in a psychiatrist's office myself."

"Hmm. You feel it is a weakness that brought you to me. Why is that?"

"Because, I must be weak or I would be able to handle this, this...whatever it is, by myself. I've always been able to cope. Even my Mom is doing better than I am.

This is so frustrating. I'm well educated and intelligent. Coping shouldn't be a problem. It's embarrassing. I just want to be better...to be myself again."

"First of all, let me tell you that in my experience, it's not weak people who sometimes break down. It's the strong ones. The ones that have shouldered their responsibilities well and have plowed through with little down time and little thought for their own wellbeing. You would be surprised at the number of highly educated, professional people that I have as clients. From what you have described, you had a very unique and close bond with your father. "

"Yes," said Rebecca. "He was my anchor and with him I was safe. I know people think of me as this tough broad who spits nails, but that's not true. The love of my Dad was the bedrock of my life. That love made me confident and sure. Now that the foundation has been pulled out from under me, I don't know what to do."

"You took a few weeks off to heal and then ploughed right back into work full force. Let me ask you...how long do you think it should take to get over a death of someone close to you?"

"I don't know, a few weeks...two months at the most?"

"And if you don't 'get over it' that quickly. What then?"

"I don't know, but I have a reputation and position to protect, dammit. Failure is not an option. Besides, I feel like I'm letting my Dad down. He would be the first to tell me to get over it."

"You've had a great shock and your system has been flooded with chemicals causing an imbalance which has produced panic attacks. No, not everyone responds the same way. This is how your body has responded. Going forward, I will teach you some strategies that should help you function while you find your feet. We'll explore why you think you're weak because you have panic attacks and why you think you have let anybody down. We'll also take a look at any other ideas you may have on what constitutes the worth of the individual. I would like to see you twice a week for counselling. We'll also put you on a small dosage of a daily anti-anxiety medication to help restore the balance in your brain. I'll also give you a prescription for Lorazepam, for the times the anxiety is overwhelming."

"Pills? No way. I don't want pills."

"Ah, I assume you think medication for emotional distress is only a crutch for those that aren't strong enough to soldier on themselves? Let me ask you...if you had a heart condition or high blood pressure, or any number of chronic diseases that require medication to help you live, would you take it?"

"Yes, but this is different. Those are physical conditions that can be measured and seen. This...this...is, I don't know what, but it's not a real illness. I just need to suck up the pain and get control again."

"Really? Not a real illness. Part of the problem with anxiety is that some people want to be in control of everything and when they can't, they feel it's an affront to their intelligence or fortitude. This is distorted thinking. It's actually very arrogant as it diminishes anyone who has an emotional or mental disorder. We will treat the deeper lying issues of this syndrome in future visits, but for immediate help or when the panic is out of control, I want you to consider the remedy I have recommended. I'm sure you'll feel much better in a few months. Sometimes behavioural modification is all that's required to set things right again. Sometimes the chemical changes are severe, but can be managed by the medication which will need to be taken for the rest of your life. We'll try gradual withdrawal after a few months to see how it goes. Following that we'll be able to determine whether or not you will require it for a longer period of time."

Chagrined, Becca reluctantly took the prescription offered to her and rose to leave the office. "I know I sound ungrateful, doctor, but I'm not. My life has been turned upside down and it's infuriating. At the moment, my brother has all the responsibility for the business and he needs me. I do look forward to working with you."

Dr. Holden smiled. "I'm sure you'll do just fine, Ms. Wainwright. I look forward to working with you as well. Please see my Assistant on your way out, to make our next appointment."

Rebecca picked up her purse and turning, exited the doctor's office. David stood and taking her hand they left the office building.

Well, this is somewhere I never thought I'd be. I wonder how long it will take.

***

Rebecca thought about how she grudgingly kept her bi-weekly sessions with Dr. Holden all the while trying new strategies to improve her outlook on life. She took the prescribed medication and found it helped a great deal to take the edge off things. The panic attacks subsided considerably, the pills allowing her to get out of the house. Little by little she was able to go to a restaurant, theatre and other events she had once enjoyed. The first time she was able to take the GO train on her own with no attack, the family had a celebration dinner. By February, she was doing so well that her counselling sessions had been reduced to once a month. Dr. Holden had gradually been weaning her from the meds, but they found the panic came back full force without them, so she reluctantly renewed her prescription. Rebecca remembered how gradually she began to feel more like her old self, although she was always on guard for the next attack. Picking up her tea cup, she put away the photo album and went upstairs to shower and change for dinner. She had so much to tell David. Just how she was going to tell him about what happened today, well, that was another question.

Chapter Twenty-Two

*L*ater that evening, after a family dinner and the girls had been put to bed; Rebecca took a glass of wine into the family room and sat on the couch near the fire. David joined her and turned on the fireplace and some soft music.

"Ah, this is great," he said stretching out in the recliner beside the couch. "I love these quiet times...just the two of us, a glass of wine, a nice fire and soft music."

Rebecca smiled at her husband. "I have something I want to talk to you about."

David sat up and leaned forward in the chair. "Mrs. Brown said you went driving today. You didn't get into an accident did you? Are you okay?"

Rebecca sighed. "Better than I've been in ages, although I did wake up in a full blown attack. Cissy came over this afternoon and we talked. That's what I want to share with you. While I was gone I came across an old stone house that's for sale near Port Perry. It's fantastic and I want to use some of the money Dad left me to buy it. I can use it as a get away.

"You've found a what," David queried?

"A house. When I was driving. It's complicated." Rebecca then proceeded to tell him all that had transpired during the day. "Cissy's coming tomorrow, we're going to spend the day at the library doing research. Later in the week, we'll drive to the Land Registry Office to find out more about the property. After that we'll drive to the Realtor's to get the key so I can show her the place. Can you come as well? I'd really like your opinion. It has an old greenhouse that could be easily repaired, plus some formal gardens and lots of space for more. You've been talking about expanding your landscape business and this could be the perfect spot. I understand this is a surprise and what I've told you sounds nuts, but I'm not crazy. That place makes me feel I belong there and I need to find out why."

David sat silently listening to Rebecca's story. He was disturbed by her tale. "Becca, what the hell are you talking about? Visions? Ghosts? Since when have you been attracted to that stuff? I know Cissy's really into it, but you've always laughed at her quirks. Dammit, it's not good for you. You're fragile enough without adding in any spooks." David stood up pacing the room and running his hand through his hair. "Bad idea. You've been stable for a while but this could destroy everything we've worked so hard for. You don't need any other place but here where we can look after you. Just leave it alone."

"See, that's what I'm talking about. Do you have any idea what it feels like to have people hovering waiting for you to break? I need a sanctuary where I can just be me... not Charles Wainwright's daughter, your wife or the girls' mother. I know I should have told you sooner what I've been thinking but this place calls to me. What occurred today happened, and I don't know why. My next appointment with Dr. Holden is soon and I'll talk to her about it. See if she has a logical explanation."

"Well I'm glad you'll talk to Dr. Holden, but why do you need to get away? Or do you mean you need to get away from me? I don't want you sick again."

"Thanks for the vote of confidence. I'm not going to get sick again. I need my own space so I can breathe. Sometimes the constant concern can be suffocating. It's my money and my life. If you can't support me, I'll go on my own," she said as she stood to walk out of the room.

"Dammit, Becca. Gimme a break. I had no idea you needed a hideaway and now you're telling me you've found one. On top of that, you inform me it's out in the boondocks and you had some weird experiences while you were there. And, you've already talked to the Realtor and Cissy. WHAT THE HELL AM I SUPPOSED TO THINK? After all we've been through this last year, I don't think it's unreasonable to be concerned, do you?"

"I'm sorry, David. Of course you're right. I only started looking today. I wasn't going behind your back. My thinking process is fine but you may not think it is. Denying my experience doesn't make it any less real and I felt Cissy would understand. Yes, I've laughed at what I call her 'woo-woo stuff' but if anyone could explain what happened to me, it'll be her. Arriving at Stone Cottage felt like coming home. This place just feels so right. "

"I wish you had at least consulted me before going off half-cocked and getting the Realtor involved. I understand you're excited, but be careful. The hallucinations can't be good for you. You'll do want you want but I don't want you going out there alone. Let me clear my calendar and I'll come with you."

***

Later as they lay in bed, Rebecca could feel the dissonance between them. Usually they were in harmony with each other's thoughts, but since the attacks started they'd gradually moved farther apart. At the moment David had his back to her. Used to falling asleep in his arms, she felt lonely. Part of it was her own fault. She had put up walls between them to shield herself from any criticism and had no idea how to break them down. Exhausted from the day's excursion, she fell into a fitful sleep. While tossing and turning, a dream came to her. There was a young woman in what appeared to be the bedroom of a wealthy home. Not the same girl that was at the pond, but a woman who looked very similar. She was dressed in old fashioned garb and the furnishings of the room were antique. The room was large, containing a bay window overlooking a garden. The atmosphere of the room was filled with anxiety and tension. Someone was in the adjoining room and her stomach started to knot. The woman climbed into the large bed. Rebecca melded with and became her. She could feel and experience everything that happened. Soon the door to the room opened and a man walked in, wearing only a dressing gown.

"Henrietta, I know that you have no experience with what goes on between a man and a woman. I want you to know that I understand you may be frightened, but I will try to be as gentle as I can. I do not wish to hurt you, but the marriage act usually hurts a woman the first time. I promise that it will not hurt after that."

What was he talking about? What hurt?

Her husband approached the bed and removed his dressing gown. Henrietta's eyes opened wide and her throat went dry. Revulsion caused her to turn her head. She wanted to go home and be with Maggie and her books. His male appendage was so large. Whatever was he going to do with that? Fear had her backing up until she was pressed against the headboard.

The man climbed into the bed and drew her into his arms. He began to place light kisses along her forehead, her cheek and down her neck. She sat rigid and still. Well, that felt nice, although it did make her feel strange down near her stomach. He unbuttoned her nightgown and placed his hand on her breast. She stiffened and pushed his hand away.

"No, my dear, don't do that. This is perfectly acceptable between married people. It is expected. Did no one explain anything to you?"

"No," replied Henrietta. "My Mother said that ladies do not speak of this kind of thing and that you would explain everything to me. She told me it was disgusting, but it would soon be over. I was told it was the only way to have children and that once I give you an heir, I wouldn't have to do it anymore. I am to lie still and do my duty."

"Oh, Henrietta, that's not true. My love, you have missed so much."

The man pulled Henrietta close and proceeded to explain to her just what was going to happen.

"You're going to do what, Jonathan?" she exclaimed. "Absolutely not! I'm sure that can't be right."

"Don't be afraid. I'll be as slow and as gentle as I can." Jonathan removed her nightgown and lay Henrietta on the bed. She was thoroughly alarmed and embarrassed. No one had seen her naked before. Her cheeks flamed and she covered her bosom with her arms. Jonathan gently took her hands and uncovered her breasts.

"You are so beautiful."

Henrietta tightened her hands into fists and lay stiff and silent while he explored every inch of her body. New sensations flooded her mind. Everywhere tingled and she felt as if she were on fire. It wasn't unpleasant, but she had no idea how to react to the way her body was responding. No one had explained to her that she would feel like this. It must be wrong. She wished he would stop.

"Open your legs for me, Henrietta."

Henrietta obediently opened her legs.

Oh, dear God, he's touching me there.

"Ah, good, you are ready for me. I am going to enter you now, my dear, and I'll be as gentle as I can."

Henrietta's body tightened in preparation for the onslaught and she shut her eyes. She could feel him at the entrance to her most private place. Tears leaked from the corners of her eyes and trickled down her cheeks. He was too big. This would never work. Hurry, hurry, hurry her mind chanted. Get this over with.

Jonathan slowly entered her body and with one thrust broke through the wall that separated the girl from the woman. Henrietta let out a scream as the pain from the tearing speared through her body, like a hot lance through soft flesh. Never had she felt such agony, fear, disgust and embarrassment all at the same time.

Jonathan lay still for a moment.

"It's all right, the pain is over and this will never hurt again. I promise."

Anger, hot and lethal, filled her senses. Oh, she hated him at that moment and this disgusting act. She felt thoroughly violated.

Get off me, you oaf.

"It will just be a little longer and soon be over. Lie still and I will finish as quickly as I can."

Finish what? Oh no, not again. I can't bear it.

Henrietta shut her eyes tightly as Jonathan pushed his phallus in and out of her vagina, until she felt him stiffen and a gush of something warm flooded her interior. Jonathan collapsed and quickly withdrew his rod.

Henrietta lay stunned. Sometime in the last five minutes she had lost sense of self. The shy, trusting girl had been mercilessly annihilated and was replaced by an angry, bitter woman. Never had she felt so humiliated. Turning on her side away from Jonathan, she curled up in the fetal position crying softly into the pillow.

"I'm sorry, Henrietta. I wish that your mother or some lady of your family had discussed these matters with you. This coupling can really be very pleasant for both people involved and it really is necessary to beget a child. Please turn over and let me wash you. The breaking of your seal incurs blood and I'm sure you would like to be clean."

Blood? What was he talking about? True, her inner thighs felt sticky, but she thought that it had come from whatever had gushed into her when he went still.

Henrietta looked down at herself and the bed. There was the blood. Completely undone she began to sob. She reached for her nightgown to cover herself and stared at her husband. "That was unspeakable. Now I know why my mother would never mention this to me. I have never felt more disgraced in my life. Please leave my room and I will tend to washing myself."

"Henrietta, I am sorry you feel that way. I promise you it will get better with time. There's nothing of which to be ashamed, you have done nothing wrong. Your body is beautiful and generous and I am delighted with it. As we get more accustomed to each other, you may find that you will actually enjoy the coupling. I will leave you now to get your rest, but I will be returning tomorrow night and every night thereafter, until you are with child." Jonathan stood, put on his dressing gown and leaned in to give his wife a kiss on the forehead. "Good night, my dear. I promise it will get better."

He walked to his own room and shut the door between them. The sounding of the closing door was like a death knell to Henrietta. Enjoy that filthy act? Not in this lifetime. She had been hoping with everything in her that she would finally have someone of her own to love, but if it involved the marriage bed, she was doomed to failure. She, who prided herself on her decorum, hated the way that he touched her body and had complete mastery over it. His touching had produced uncontrollable sensations and they frightened her. She climbed out of the bed and went to the washstand. After cleaning herself, she went to sit in the window seat to look out at the garden. This was such a lovely old house and she had wanted desperately to find happiness here, but now was afraid that wasn't going to happen. Hopefully, once she produced an heir, and they didn't have to do that act anymore, they could become friends. The tearing of her nether regions had also torn a hole in her heart and she was very afraid it would never be mended.

"No," cried Rebecca thrashing about in the bed.

David quickly put his arms around her. "Becca, wake up. You're having a bad dream."

Rebecca opened her eyes and turning her head to David's shoulder sobbed.

Oh my God! What was that? It was so real. I can still feel Henrietta's pain, humiliation and anxiety.

She explained to David what she had dreamt. "What a horrible way to start a marriage. That poor girl, what kind of mother did she have that wouldn't explain things to her? The man in the dream, he was a younger version of the one I saw today at the pond. What did this dream have to do with my experience at that house? Something very strange is going on and somehow I'm connected. I have to figure it out, David, I have to."

She got out of bed and crossed to a table in the room. Picking up a pen and pad, she wrote down to whole dream. Henrietta and Jonathan. Who were they and what was their connection to Stone Cottage and the McBrides? Putting the pad down, Rebecca climbed back into bed. David wrapped his arms around her and drew her close. His gentleness soothed her troubled mind as she slowly slid into a dreamless sleep.

Chapter Twenty-Three

$\mathcal{T}$he next morning, Rebecca drove to Cissy's home. On their way to the library, she told her about the dream. "It was so incredibly real. Somehow, I was there and experienced everything Henrietta felt. Jonathan and Henrietta. He was a younger version of the man in my hallucination with Victoria and Maddy. If Jonathan was 'Grandpa' then Henrietta must be 'Grandma'. Well, at least we have two more names on our list. "

Arriving at the library, Rebecca and Cissy met with the librarian in charge of the archives. When they explained that they were looking for background information on a William and Victoria McBride who lived in the Whitby area around the 1870's, they were led to a section of the library that had diaries, newspaper clippings, historical family records and such.

After spending hours poring over the papers, Cissy found a newspaper article listing the marriage of a William McBride and a Victoria Anne Smythe-Stratton. There was a picture of the wedding couple attached to the clipping.

"Rebecca, look. I've found something."

Rebecca joined her friend. "Oh my God, that's the young woman I saw at the pond! I don't recognize the man, though."

Cissy held the clipping in her hand. It read:

> Saturday, April 14, 1870
> was a glorious spring day
> for the wedding of Mr.
> William McBride and the
> lovely Victoria Anne
> Smythe-Stratton. The
> bride is the only child of

Mr. and Mrs. Jonathan Smythe-Stratton of England. Mrs. Smythe-Stratton is the former Lady Henrietta Easthope. Mr. McBride is a successful stone mason in the area and built his wife a lovely stone house near Port Perry.

The bride was dressed in a three piece gown made of ivory silk faille. It had a fitted bodice with fine silk lining and stays, button front with all of the buttons and trimmings being a soft blue that matched her eyes, silk cord soutash, trimmings on the bodice and overskirt, and hand lace ruffles along the shoulders with big pagoda sleeves. The underskirt had a gathered area in the rear to accommodate the bustle and an extravagantly long train. The wedding was held at All Saints Anglican Church in Briar's Mills.

The happy couple had a sumptuous wedding breakfast at the home of the bride's parents and then left for their new residence.

The ladies looked at each other in astonishment.

"Jonathan and Henrietta. Those are the names from my dream. Victoria Anne McBride was the name on the tombstone. These have to be the right people. Henrietta is Victoria's mother. By the looks of this article, the Smythe-Strattons must have been fairly high up in society if Henrietta was Lady Henrietta Easthope. Let's see if we can find out anything about them."

Cissy and Rebecca began searching with a new vigour. They discovered that the Smythe-Strattons were high enough in society to have a lot of information about them saved in the archives. Their arrival in 1855; the birth and death of their son in an influenza epidemic; the wedding of their daughter Victoria Anne to Mr. William McBride; various social functions held by Henrietta were all documented. They found mention of them in the local who's who of the time period. After exhausting all of the resources of the library, they went back to Rebecca's house to draw out a timeline for the information they had collected. Sitting in the Rebecca's study, they pulled up the spreadsheet of the information they had previously collected and added the new data to it.

"You must admit there is something more than coincidence at work here, Becca."

"Yeah, well, all I know is it feels weird. Why on earth did I feel compelled to drive up that laneway the other day? Somehow I'm connected to that place and the people that lived there, but how? I wanted a quiet place to get away by myself for a while to continue healing. How's this place supposed to help with that? The visions, ghosts or whatever, only make my anxiety worse. Shit. It's definitely real, the picture in the library proves that, but it doesn't make any sense in my world."

"I don't know why you were drawn to this place or what any of it could mean to help you get better, but it has to mean something. I was thinking. How would you feel about asking a medium to come to the house to verify what you saw?"

"Uh...no. Bunch of phonies taking advantage of gullible people."

"You're still on that track? Move on...better yet, why the hell don't you do this search by yourself? You certainly don't need my help."

"I'm sorry, Cissy. Knee-jerk reaction. You know how uncomfortable I am with metaphysical stuff. You're right. I'll think about it. If I can't find answers in a practical way, then maybe I'll go your route."

"Okay, we'll leave it for now. Let's see how our visit to the house goes."

Chapter Twenty-Four

*W*hile at the library, Rebecca and Cissy had discovered some of Henrietta's diaries. Since ladies in the 1800's were not allowed to speak openly about their feelings or ideas, it was customary for them to keep diaries - which gave an intimate look at the daily life, frustrations, joys and sorrows of mid nineteenth century. Rebecca saw that the dates on the diaries ranged from before the Smythe-Stratton's emigrated to when Victoria got married. Requesting permission from the librarian, she made photocopies of some of the entries so that she could read them at home.

After compiling the new information, Rebecca drove Cissy home. She was eager to start reading the diary entries, so declined Cissy's invitation come in. Racing back to her house, she made her way to the sunroom and her favourite chaise. Picking up a legal pad to jot down any notes on what was written, she then read the first entry. It was dated May 5, 1855.

> We have arrived at our new home in Briar's Mills. Oh, how I hate this place. First, that horrible sea crossing which seemed to take forever; then hours in a cramped, smelly old coach and now this god forsaken backwater. Jonathan will certainly have to purchase a proper vehicle, if he expects me to accompany him anywhere. Surely there will be someone who will have a decent coach and pair that will be suitable for us. At least the main street of the village has a

number of shops and dwellings which appear to be clean and tidy. The Royal Victoria is the only hotel in the area. We will spend a few days here before moving to our estate. There are a number of businesses along with the hotel and they seem to be relatively prosperous. There are also two churches, so I presume that the citizens are somewhat civilized.

There were a group of men waiting on the front steps of the hotel when we arrived, to welcome us to their town. Jonathan told me they were the Mayor, President of the Bank, Editor of the newspaper and the representatives of the clergy. I was purposely clothed head to toe in the latest fashion from Paris. I heard a few gasps and uttered 'ohs' and 'ahs', and smiled inwardly at the gauche manners of the crowd. I might as well get them used to quality at the start so that they know what they are dealing with. Of course, Jonathan picked up Victoria and carried her from the carriage. As if she couldn't walk. He spoils that child. He stopped to chat and shake hands with the men present, before coming to look after me.

He informed me that we would be staying in town for a few days, as our manor house wasn't quite ready. Apparently, Lord Ecklesby's youngest son came over in '51 and built a lovely home just on the outskirts of town. He assured me that it is a fitting manor house on a large property surrounded by a stone wall with gates at the entrance. Ecklesby met with a riding accident two years past and the house has been vacant ever since. Hollister has seen to its purchase and hired a working crew to have it ship shape by the time we arrived. We will go tomorrow and view the house and grounds, and then I can set about hiring the household staff required. Our furniture and goods should arrive by the end of the week and we'll be all set to move in. Thank goodness, Maggie and Nanny were willing to come with us. I don't know what I should do without them. It is our new home and I will have to make the best of it. He told me there are other well educated, refined families living here that have emigrated to start afresh. Have some parties to get acquainted, he said. He'll have Hollister inquire discreetly who I would consider the best people and in time he assures me I will be the most sought after hostess in the area. We are not that far from the city of Toronto. I am allowed take the carriage and visit all of the sites they have. The new railway should be through in a year and that will make the city even closer. In fact, he will be dealing with many of the businesses there and will be required to visit for extended periods of time. Hollister has already found a lovely home on Jarvis Street, where most of the affluent members of society reside. I will be able to entertain to my heart's content. Toronto hosts a number of theatres, museums and libraries as well as a fine University. It is not a backwater but a prosperous enlightened city. He says I'll be just fine. That's all well and good for him, but what will become of me? I am afraid of this wild land and the people who live here, but I'll never let him know that. I'll show him. I will be the most sought after hostess around here. I will have the best that his money can buy. He will regret the day he took me from my home and all I know and love.

Rebecca put down the pages of the diary and picked up her legal pad. She wanted to write down her impressions of Henrietta.

I wonder why she married him, poor woman. Obviously, she hadn't wanted to emigrate and 'start afresh' as Jonathan put it.

Chapter Twenty-Five

*E*arly on Tuesday morning, Rebecca, Cissy and David set out to visit the old house. Before getting into the car, Rebecca pulled Cissy aside. "Cissy, I'm a bit worried about what will happen once we get to the house today. I've told David about the hallucinations and I'm worried if I have any more episodes like last time, he'll explode. He's already upset with me for talking to you and the Realtor before him. The dream didn't help either. I don't need any more cracks in our marriage than we already have."

"Rebecca, you've had a rough time over the last year and a half, but you're not crazy. There is an explanation for what happened. There must be a connection to the people who used to live here. Why else they appear to you? Then that dream about Henrietta and Jonathan. Even the names were correct. After we finish with the Land Registry Office, we'll go to the property and see if we can get David to go off by himself. That way, you can show me the places where you had your visions and if anything happens he won't see it and get upset."

"I'm hoping my experiences were just a onetime thing and that nothing will happen today. David wants me to see Dr. Holden about what happened. I have one more appointment with her soon, so I've told him I'll bring it up.

"That's a good idea. It will ease his mind to get her take on them. What's Dr. Holden's spiritual view on life? Is she open to alternative explanations of events, do you know?"

"Nope. It's never come up. Should be interesting to hear what she has to say."

Arriving at the Land Registry Office they discovered that a Mr. George McBride had received a land grant of one hundred acres of land in the area of Port Perry in 1840. In 1852 he had parcelled it to his four sons and himself, giving each twenty acres. One of the sons listed was a Mr. Uilleam (William) McBride. After checking the lot number they found it was the same piece of land that Rebecca was interested in.

Finishing at the Land Registry Office, they drove to the Realtor's to pick up the key. Travelling up Highway 12 Rebecca found the side road she had been looking for. Creeping along the road she spotted the 'for sale' sign and they were soon parked in the circular driveway. Getting out of the car, they stood looking at the house.

"Well, what do you think?"

"It's a lovely old building, Becca. I can see why you are drawn to it," replied David.

"See the greenhouse? I think it could be fixed up for you and the perennial garden is just beyond that."

"Huh, that looks interesting. Mind if I wander over to take a look? Will you be okay?"

"I'm fine David. Cissy is with me. You go ahead. There are a couple of other places I want to show her anyway."

"All right, if you're sure. Call if you need me."

As David sauntered off, Rebecca turned to Cissy. "Well, do you feel anything?" she asked, her own heart pounding.

"No, I do have a sense of sadness. Loneliness maybe is a better word. Are you feeling anything this time?"

"Yeah, I feel it's pulling me in...like it's welcoming me home. Let's walk down to the pond and I'll show you the grave."

Rebecca and Cissy strolled to the small hill. They stopped at the crest and Rebecca pointed out the willow tree and the pond. "There, just on the other side of the tree. You can just see the corner of the bench."

The women walked down to the tree. Rebecca could hear a soft buzzing in her head and again a sense of sadness enveloped her. Not quite as potent as last time, but still there.

"You okay? Are you sure you want to go on?" asked Cissy, concerned because her friend had gone quite pale and her movements were jerky.

"Yes, I'm fine. Better than I was last time, although I feel the sadness again."

The companions walked to the far side of the tree and Cissy saw the old grave. She walked over to it and read the inscriptions. "Well, from what we read at the library, the baby is the daughter of William and Victoria. The inscription says that Victoria passed away a few days after the baby. I don't see a grave for William and there wasn't much on him in the archives. I wonder what happened to him, and where he's buried."

They walked over and sat down on the bench.

"There's such a sense of sadness in this spot. Their loss was so great that the energy resonates even after a hundred years. Let's go into the house so we can snoop around and see if you have another reaction. If it was a ghost you saw, I still think we should get a medium out here to verify what you've discovered. I have a good friend I could call."

"Let's see what happens today. It still could be my imagination."

Cissy snorted and shook her head. "Ah, hell, Becca. Pretty vivid imagination. Anyway, my friend may be able to pick up some of the residual energy left by whatever happened here. Give us a better feel for the place and an understanding of the people involved. You've always trusted me when I've introduced you to my spiritual friends. Trust me now and I think we'll find out whatever it is we're supposed to and if there is anything we can do about it."

"I know. It's just weird thinking about a spirit. This is so far out of my comfort zone. It's hard to change my mind even when confronted with evidence to the contrary. I don't want there to be a ghost. I just want my life back to normal, but for some reason, that's not going to happen anytime soon. C'mon I'll show you the house. Then we can take the key back to the Realtor and decide what to do next."

The women stood up and walked back to the house, each lost in their own thoughts about the day. David joined them a few moments later. "This is a lovely spot, Rebecca. I'm sorry I came down on you so hard the other night but I'm worried about you...about us. If this place gives you comfort then I won't stand in your way. Thinking practically, you may be right. I am planning to expand the business, but haven't gotten around to thinking of where we could go. This place would be work very nicely. It'll take a little effort to spruce it up, but it'll be fun. We can increase the store in our current space and use these gardens to supply new varieties of stock. It'll make a great addition to where we are and a great getaway place as well. I think the girls will like it. Let's see the inside. I'd like to have a home inspection before you buy it, but it looks like a sound investment to me."

The trio walked through the house. David decided to start at the top of the house and work his way down. Rebecca said that she and Cissy would go into the living room as she wanted to show her the view from the windows. The two ladies entered the room and Rebecca showed Cissy where the ghost had appeared the last time she was here. There was no ghost today, but as they stood talking about the Spirit, mist began to fill the room.

Rebecca watched as another scene presented itself to her. Again, the room was decorated in mid nineteenth century decor. There were two women in the room seated on the couch. Beside the couch was a baby cradle. The young woman was the ghost from the previous sighting, who Rebecca now knew was Victoria. The other woman was an older but identical version of the Henrietta of her dream. Henrietta was dressed in a blue travelling cloak as if she had just arrived. The dog was beside Victoria. Henrietta was speaking.

"Well, Victoria, it seems that you too are destined to repeat that disgusting marriage act as I had too. Tsk, tsk. It's such a shame that Madeleine is a girl."

Shocked by Henrietta's attitude, and trying to keep her anger in check, Victoria spoke.

"Mother, I love Maddy more than anything alive. I am delighted with her just the way she is. As far as the marriage act is concerned, I will tell you that I am delighted in the way Will loves me and do not think it disgusting at all."

Henrietta jumped to her feet, a look of astonishment etched on her face.

"Victoria, I am appalled by your attitude. Has being married to a common man and moving away from my influence made you into a wanton?"

Victoria sighed. She had so hoped that a grandbaby would soften her mother, but she could see that wasn't going to happen. She stood, straightened her shoulders and looked her mother in the eye.

"Mother, I will only tell you this one time. I will not have you speak about my person or my family in that way. My husband is not common, but the epitome of a gentleman. I am not a wanton but a happily married woman and the mother of a beautiful little girl. I am deeply sorry, but if you cannot accept these terms, you are not welcome in my home."

Henrietta drew herself up to her full height and turning on her heel strode out of the house.

"Becca. Rebecca. Can you hear me?"

The mist cleared and Rebecca was once again standing in the empty room with Cissy. "What...What just happened?

"I don't know except that you went very still and white. I couldn't get your attention. You frightened me. Obviously, you saw something. Did the ghost appear again?"

Rebecca told Cissy what had transpired. "Henrietta was furious with her daughter. Her attitude jibes with my reaction to her diary entry. She didn't appear to want her daughter in her writings and the way she spoke to her just now confirms it. Poor Victoria, I feel sorrier for her now than I did before. Although, in Henrietta's defense, when I dreamt about her she was in such pain and humiliation because of sex. It must have tainted her view of life. I wonder if she was ever happy."

They left the living room and met David in the foyer. He was pleased with how well the house had been kept up and Rebecca was relieved that he appeared enthusiastic about purchasing it. They drove back to the Realtor's to return the key. Mr. Addison greeted them. They all entered his office and took a seat.

"Did you find everything to your satisfaction?"

"Yes, we did."

"Good. Just to let you know, the dwelling itself has been renovated over the years. Electricity was added and brought up to code. It's heated with propane, so there's no problem there. New towers have been built so internet and cell phone signals are available. The roof was redone in 2012, and the carriage house has been turned into a garage that will hold three cars. Here are the property taxes for last year. The forest area was turned over to the Conservancy, which brings the taxes down considerably. It's a nice, snug little place and reasonably priced.   Is there anything else you want to know?"

"Not at the moment," replied Rebecca. "We'd like to have a home inspection done before we make an offer. Please make the arrangements and draw up the papers."

"Certainly,   I will let you know as soon as everything is ready."

"Oh, there is one thing...has anyone ever mentioned a ghost in the house?"

Mr.   Addison   stroked   his   chin   and   looked thoughtful.

"I think there was a rumour that went around a few years back. I mentioned in our phone conversation the author who rented the cottage for the summer to do some writing. He came into the office before even a week was out, saying he thought the house must be haunted as on several occasions he heard a dog whining. Apparently, he was quite freaked out. He left the key and never went back. That was before my time here, but, other than that, I've never heard anyone mention it. Is that a problem?"

"No, no problem. Just curious. Thank you for your time. I look forward to hearing from you soon."

As they walked to the car, Rebecca turned to Cissy and whispered. "Shit. Not what I wanted to hear., another verification of the dog. You win. I might not like or want it, but I have to admit something very strange going on and it's connected to that house."

Chapter Twenty-Six

*U*pon returning home, Rebecca went to the sunroom to read another of Henrietta's diary entries. She wanted to know more about this woman and why she was so upset with her daughter. She retrieved the notes from Henrietta's wedding day to see if she could understand her better. She read.

> June 16, 1850. My wedding day. I am so frightened. Everyone thinks it is a splendid match, but I'm not so sure. Is it a 'splendid match'? This marriage will certainly save the family from disaster. Mother is mortified that her future son-in-law is a cit, but Father had assured her it was the only way we can refill our coffers after he lost most of our fortune in a gambling hell. This marriage will allow them to carry on as if nothing had happened, and no one will be the wiser. In return, Mr. Smythe-Stratton will make the business contacts he needs in the upper class. Satisfaction all around. It is just that I had hoped to marry for love. I respect him, but that's not love, is it? Maybe, in time it will be, and then everyone will be happy. At least, I still have all of my family and friends nearby. I still have Maggie as well. I know she's only a servant and we shouldn't be so close, but I don't know what I would do without her. She's the only person I can talk to and

she's my closest friend, although if Mother knew she'd be appalled. I don't care. Maggie is mine and I won't allow The Countess to spoil our friendship. Thank goodness she is going with me after I'm married. Nothing much will change, will it?

Rebecca closed her eyes and thought about what she had read. Henrietta had been an innocent pawn in her parents' plans. She knew that arranged marriages were the norm of the day, but she had never really thought about it before. How humiliating to be sold off to the highest bidder to save the family fortune. She picked up the next entry and read further.

Well, it's over. I am no longer Lady Henrietta Easthope, daughter of the Earl and Countess of Rathbourne, but Henrietta Smythe-Stratton, wife of the wealthy Jonathan Smythe-Stratton. At least the ceremony went well and Mother was pleased. That may very well be the first time I have ever heard her say something pleasant to me. I was absolutely shocked at her gift this morning. After I was ready she said. 'Hmmm. Well, at least you are dressed in the latest fashion. I have something that will make you sparkle.' Then she gave me a beautiful sapphire necklace. Placing it around my neck, she said, 'There. That looks quite lovely and definitely enhances your gown. Wear it with pride, my dear, as you come from a long list of England's greatest families. My only regret is that you will not have a title to go with it, but such is life.' I was stunned. I do wish she hadn't added that last bit. She just can't let go of the fact that I am not marrying into the ton. I asked her, what about my happiness? Doesn't that count? What if I don't wish to wed? She was mortified. Unthinkable, nonsense. Of course I wish to be married. She was sorry that after all of the seasons I'd had there were no offers from a wealthy lord. She said that I was not exactly a 'diamond of the first water' like, Elizabeth, but she had hoped with Father's connections and my excellent training, one of the titled members of the ton would have taken a fancy to me. Elizabeth again. Of course I'd be compared to her. My sister is so beautiful and that appears to be the only thing of which my Mother approves. She will make a brilliant match, I'm sure. Now that the Earl and Countess have the money, they'll be able to give her a proper season. Blah. Mother will never know how much she hurt me with her talk of Elizabeth and her splendid match. I've done everything I can to please her and make her love me, but it was never enough. I'm only a means to an end for her precious Elizabeth. I'm surprised she didn't save the necklace for her. I was so happy with it when she gave it to me. Now it feels like the iron shackle of an animal being led to slaughter. I hate it. It's the end of what little freedom I did have and the beginning of servitude to a husband of which my family is ashamed. But I can't let her know."

Rebecca put down the pages. How humiliating to be constantly compared to a younger and more beautiful sister.

I wonder how Elizabeth's life did turn out. Did she make her 'brilliant match'. That would really have been hard on Henrietta. Too bad she never got any enjoyment from sex. That would have helped.

Rebecca shuffled through the diary entries and picked up another one regarding the sex talk between the Countess and Henrietta.

I'm just about to leave for my new home, but Mother had called me aside to give me instructions on how to be a good wife. 'About the marriage act, Henrietta. I should probably have talked to you earlier, but it is not something that is discussed in civilized society. I don't wish to discuss it any further. Mr. Smythe-Stratton will instruct you later. Do your duty, girl, and everything will be fine.' The marriage act... What was that? I have overheard some girls giggling about men at one of the soirees. They had talked about stolen kisses in the gardens. Mr. Smythe-Stratton has only kissed my hand. A tingly sensation coursed through my body. It wasn't unpleasant, but it frightened me. I felt like I was losing control and I will not allow that. I cannot give in to my emotions. I did once. I started to cry and thought I'd never stop. My eyes were puffy and my skin was all blotchy. Mother was mortified and kept me locked in my room for two days to think about my 'lack of decorum'. Never again will I allow myself to be put in that position. The girls at the party were talking about kissing on the mouth and touching the body, but that can't be right. I wish I had an older sister or someone I can talk to. How I wish I didn't have to go through with this, whatever 'this' is.   I want to stay here with Maggie and my books. I'm so scared. I can't do this, I just can't.

Rebecca put the diary down. Tears formed in her eyes.

Ah, so that explains it.   No wonder she was so frightened of sex. She had known nothing of it before her marriage and the Countess sure hadn't helped. What a bitch. It's a shame that Jonathan couldn't have helped her more.   I understand her a little better now, but I still wonder why she disliked her daughter so much.

Chapter Twenty-Seven

A few days later, Rebecca had her final visit with Dr. Holden. She was a little nervous about the doctor's reaction to her experiences. She entered the office and sat in her usual chair.

"Rebecca, how good it is to see you. You are looking very well, how are you feeling?"

"Much better thank you, Doctor."

"What's been happening since the last time I saw you? How are you coping with the anxiety?"

"I'm really pleased to tell you that the panic attacks have almost stopped. I had one, last month, but nothing since then. I keep my lorazepam on hand if they should occur and with my anti-anxiety meds and the coping strategies I've learned, I truly feel better."

"That's wonderful. We'll continue to monitor your medication through your regular doctor, but due to your progress, I feel that we can dispense with any further counselling sessions."

"That is good news, but I do have something I wish to discuss with you today."

Rebecca then explained all that had happened to her in the months between visits.

"So you see, I don't know why I'm seeing these apparitions. Do you have any logical explanation for them? Have you ever encountered this type of hallucination before?"

"Why do you assume they are hallucinations? I have seen and heard many strange things in the course of my practice over the years. Can you not accept these happenings at face value?"

"But that would mean that ghosts exist."

"Is that so hard to consider? Do you believe in angels or an afterlife?"

"Well, yes. That's what I was taught. But ghosts? Not so good. Cissy has tried to encourage me to broaden my horizons, but I've never felt inclined to do so."

"In my experience, there is much more to this world than what we feel with our five senses. You've told me that you practice yoga and have tried to meditate to help with your stress. I would encourage you to explore a little more. You may discover a whole new way of living that will add richness to your life."

"So, you don't think I'm digressing?"

"No, Rebecca, I don't. You are very sane. You have never been crazy. Yes, you have an anxiety disorder, but that's easily handled with the medication and your coping strategies. You are definitely not certifiable."

"That's a relief. Cissy wants to bring a Medium out to the house. I'm not at all sure about that, but maybe it's worth a try."

"Why not? You may be surprised at what you'll find. Challenge what you've been taught. That's what helps us grow and learn. Come and see me again in six months. I'd like to know the outcome of your discovery."

"Thank you Doctor. I will. And thank you for all your help over the last year. I'll be sure to let you know what happens."

Arriving home, Rebecca called Cissy. "I've just come from Dr. Holden's office. I told her about my experiences and what we discovered and she doesn't think I'm crazy at all."

"I agree. What else did she say?"

"She thought it would be okay to have the Medium come out to the house to verify what I've seen. Can you arrange it?"

"Yes, of course. I have one friend who's helped the police on certain missing person cases and he's very good. I'll give him a call and see what we can arrange."

Cissy contacted her friend, Robert Wilson. He agreed to come out to the house and take a look around. Robert was a well-known Medium in the Greater Toronto Area whom Cissy had known for a long time. She had seen some amazing things that he had done and she trusted him. On the next sunny Saturday morning, Robert drove out to Stone Cottage. He was about forty, tall, with an athletic build. He was dressed in blue jeans, a Tee shirt and leather loafers.

Well, he doesn't look like a phoney.

"I hear there might be something going on with the house," he said as he approached Rebecca.

"Well, something's happening, but I'm not sure what."

"Yeah, Cissy mentioned you weren't keen on the idea of ghosts."

"I haven't been, but now I'm not so sure."

"Okay, let's see what we have."

"No offense, Mr. Wilson, but if there are such things as ghosts, I'm not sure they interact with the living. I don't trust Mediums. I think most of them are frauds preying on vulnerable people but Cissy says you're legit, so we'll give it a try."

"No offense taken, Ms. Wainwright. There are some people trying to make a quick buck off of others pain. That's not me. Please, call me Rob. Shall we get this show on the road?"

"Rebecca, and thanks. Yeah, let's go."

He scanned the outside of the building. "Interesting. I sense both a great happiness, but great tragedy as well. Lots of love and laughter, but a deep despair overlaying it. Well, let's go in, shall we? I'll see what I can pick up."

No kidding, Sherlock. Any place this old will have both happiness and sadness. What a waste of time, thought Rebecca.

The trio made their way into the house. Standing in the foyer, Rob stood still and closed his eyes. Taking a deep breath, he imbibed the essence of the house. An acrid, crisp electrical smell assaulted his nose. He had learned to associate this particular odour, which was similar to the top of a battery, with houses that contained an earthbound spirit. From his experience, he knew that no one else could smell it. Moving around the room, he found the strongest aroma near the living room door.

"I'd like to start in this room," he said.

"No problem," replied Rebecca.

She and Cissy preceded Rob into the room. He stood just inside the door for a few minutes and then walked to the window and stood looking out.

"I sense a female presence here, looking out of this window. She's young and searching for something...no...*someone*. Right. She's waiting. There's another being with her. Not a person, but spirit." He was silent for a few minutes, eyes closed and brow furrowed. "Was there another apparition in the room with the female spirit you saw, Rebecca?"

Uh-oh, the dog again. "Yes"

Rob opened his eyes and looked down. "What on earth? Hey, old boy, where did you come from? Whose dog is this? I didn't hear him come in."

Rebecca and Cissy looked at each other.

"What dog?"

"The one right here."

Cissy looked at him in astonishment. Rebecca had already seen the animal come into the room, so she knew what he was seeing.

"Ummm, Rob, there's no dog," said Cissy.

"Well, well," chuckled Rob. He crouched down to scratch the creature, which promptly disappeared. Standing, he turned to the women and said. "I see. That's the other spirit I was sensing. He stayed behind to protect his mistress. How delightful. I haven't run across a situation like this in a long time. I wasn't expecting an animal. I'd forgotten they do sometimes stay until they're sure their owners are okay. He's not going to cross until she does. That's all I'm getting, Rebecca. You definitely have a very lonely wraith. She's sad, frightened and waiting. Unless someone convinces her that she is dead and needs to cross over into the light, she will remain here. There doesn't appear to be anyone or anything else, but we can go through the rest of the house, if you like, just to make sure."

Rebecca's skin was tingling as Rob spoke. He couldn't know what she had seen. Cissy must have told him. She looked at Cissy.

"I know what you're thinking, but I didn't tell him anything."

Rob smiled at her.

"No, Rebecca. Cissy didn't coach me. The presence really is here. I've witnessed countless scenarios involving spirits who are stuck on this plane. For her to have appeared to you, suggests that somehow you are connected."

"Thank you Rob. I had to make sure. What you saw is exactly what I see. A young woman with a dog, looking out of the window. I also saw the animal today when you did. What I want to know is why. Why doesn't anyone else see her, except you and me?"

"Perhaps you knew one another in different lifetime. If you want to search further along those lines, I do know a couple of very good past life regressionists that I would be happy to recommend."

"Whoa that's out of my comfort zone. I'm just getting used to the idea that ghosts exist and there's one in this house, but a connection from another life?"

"It certainly is one explanation of what's happening. There could be others. This ghost definitely has some unfinished business on this plane. Until she can resolve it, she will always be stuck. Since you are the only one who can see her, somehow you have the key to getting her to move on."

"I've been taught that we only have this one life and that's it. Then we go on to our eternal reward or punishment. I've never even given past lives a thought. Of course, I've heard about them, just like everyone else, but always assigned it to eastern mysticism and that's just not my thing. I'm really going to have to think long and hard about this."

"I understand. New paradigms can be difficult to wrap your head around, but you might just find your answer if you do a little more exploring outside your normal range of experience. There's lots of good research out there. Talk to Cissy and if you decide you would like to pursue the past life avenue, I will send her the names of the people I told you about. It's been nice meeting you, Rebecca and I really hope you can find satisfactory answers to your questions."

With that, Rob said his farewells and drove off the property.

Rebecca turned to Cissy. "You said you didn't tell him anything and I could see the dog this afternoon when he bent down to pat him. I guess I have to admit there's something to this ghost business."

"Don't sound so miserable," Cissy teased. "I've known him for a long time and think he's one of the best I've met. He's always had this ability, although he didn't think it was a gift when he was a kid. He thought that everyone could see spirits and I guess it must have really freaked out his family when he would talk about playing with another kid that they couldn't see. As he grew older, he learned when to say something and when to keep quiet. He's been helping other people for about twenty years now and really enjoys the work."

"Well, he certainly didn't look like what I assumed would be a typical medium. I would have run for the hills if you had presented me with Madame Whatshername decked out in a purple turban with plumes and rhinestones," she laughed.

"Could you really see me having someone like that show up?" Cissy snickered. "Seriously, though, he did describe the woman and dog. He was also right about you being really attached to this place. So, where do we go from here?"

Chapter Twenty-Eight

$\mathcal{V}$ictoria Anne sighed.

That woman was here again. I wish she had stayed. I would like to talk to her. I wonder if she knows where Will is.

She needed to feel his arms around her, she loved his gentle touch. Her Mother had tried to explain what would happen on their wedding night. Annie remembered what she had said to her just before they left for the wedding.

"What will happen tonight is something all married women must endure. The first time will hurt, but it is tolerable after that. Give him a son and he'll leave you alone. I wish you well, Victoria. May you be happy."

Annie had never understood why her mother would say something like that. Did she not enjoy being loved by her husband? Maybe that's why she seemed so angry all the time. Will was a wonderful lover and Annie smiled as she remembered their wedding night. Never had she felt more loved and cherished than she did then. She pictured it in her mind.

After their wedding, they had travelled to an inn about halfway to their new home. Holding hands, they made their way to the room allotted to them and closed the door. Annie took off her cloak, bonnet and gloves and set them on the chair in the room. Walking over to the window, she looked out at the street below. Will came up behind her and put his arms around her waist and kissed her neck. She leaned back into him.

"Everything feels so different and yet it all feels the same. This morning, I was Miss Victoria Anne Smythe-

Stratton, a young innocent girl, and tonight I am Mrs. William McBride. Still young and innocent, for the moment, but changed as well."

Will chuckled.

"Well, let's see what we can do about the innocent part. I'm sure that I am up to the challenge."

He turned her in his arms and lowering his head kissed her gently. Longing stirred in his loins and he deepened the kiss. Sliding his tongue along the opening of her mouth, he pried it open and slid his tongue inside. Annie gasped and pulled back her head.

"It's all right, my love. Do you not like it?"

"I think so. My insides are on fire and every inch of me is tingling."

"Oh, Annie, there is so much more to feel and enjoy. I can't wait to show you. I know it's a little early, but will you come to bed now?"

"Yes, my love. I want to know and to feel everything you want to share with me. Show me what it is to be a woman."

Will started with the buttons on her dress pausing only long enough to take small nips and kisses along her neck and shoulders. With the buttons undone, he lifted Annie's arms and removed her frock letting it fall to the floor. Standing only in her undergarments, she tried to cover herself.

"No, my sweet, don't be embarrassed. It is perfectly all right for me to see you like this. You are my wife and what happens between us belongs to us and no one else."

"No one has ever seen me without my dress , it feels strange."

"Do you need help to remove the rest of your clothing?"

"No, I can do it myself, but can we close the curtains to make it darker?"

"I would rather look at you in the fading daylight, but it you are uncomfortable, we can wait until nightfall."

"No...I...I...want to go on but I'm scared. So many thoughts and feelings are swirling around in my head and body; I don't know what to do. But, I trust you and our love."

Annie slowly removed the rest of her underclothes and dropped them on top of her dress. Finally, all barriers between them were gone and Annie was naked and free. Will stepped back and just looked at her. The setting sun was shining into the room, casting Annie with a golden glow as if she'd been sprinkled by fairy dust.

"You are so beautiful," he whispered blinded by her and so full of yearning that his throat constricted and he could say no more.

"Nobody's seen me naked before," said Annie, wonder sounding in her voice. "I'm happy you find my body pleasing."

With a groan, Will drew her close.

"You are much more than pleasing. Will you let me show you how I feel?"

He kissed her starting with her forehead and running small kisses down the side of her face to her neck and then to her mouth. Taking her mouth, his tongue swept the inside and did a tango with her tongue. She pulled back and looked him in the eye.

"First, I would look at you. I have never seen a man's body before."

Will stepped back from her.

"Would you care to do the honours?"

Annie stepped forward and biting her lower lip began to undo the buttons on his shirt. She removed it and moved on to his pants. As she started to unbutton the first button, she hesitated.

"It's all right, mo ghraidh. You are my wife now and it is perfectly acceptable for you to see me naked."

~ 157 ~

She continued on and soon Will was as naked as she. She looked over his body from head to toe, stopping at his groin.

"Oh, my," she exclaimed her hand flying to her mouth. "I have seen the stallions that my father owns when they are ready to mate, but I have never seen a man before. What the stallion does to the mare...is that what a man and a woman do?"

Will chuckled.

"Yes, but it will be fine I assure you."

"But... that won't fit in me, will it?"

"Yes, and it will bring you so much pleasure that I'm sure you'll keep me busy all night. So much so that I'm sure that I won't be able to leave the bed tomorrow to journey on home. Come. I'll show you what I mean."

Annie took his hand and they walked to the bed. She lay down, stiff as a board, a worried frown on her face. Will climbed in beside her and stroked the frown lines on her forehead.

"Don't worry; I will be as gentle as possible. It may hurt when I break through your barrier, but after that there will be no pain. Your body will stretch to accommodate me. I want you to shut your eyes and just enjoy the sensations you feel. That's it...relax."

Will began to stroke her torso, kissing the frown and her eyelids and moving his mouth to hers. She tasted like apple cinnamon, sweet, tart and spicy all at the same time. His hands stroked up and down her arms, gradually moving up to cup one breast. Annie's eyes flew open and her limbs stiffened. She gave a small gasp.

"It's okay. Close your eyes and just savor how wonderful you feel with my caresses," He murmured.

Annie let her eyelids close as Will continued to brush her breasts with his fingers. So incredibly soft, he thought. Her skin feels like the gossamer wings of a butterfly. He had wanted to touch and taste her since that first morning in the garden. Trying hard to remember to go slowly, his own passion threatened to overwhelm him.

Annie felt a pleasurable pressure begin to build in the area below her stomach and between her legs. Will cupped one breast in his hand. Lowering his mouth to the straining nipple, he began to suckle. Annie's body lifted off the bed, the exquisite sensation creating a wave of intense pleasure. Her mind pleaded for more. She was a mixture of raw emotion and pure pleasure, combined with a desperate longing - for what she didn't know. Drowning in ecstasy, she thought she would die.

Sending feather light strokes up and down her body with his fingers, Will's mouth turned its attention to the other breast. Gently and repeatedly he tugged on the teat with his teeth. Letting go, he lapped at the breast with his tongue tasting the special nectar that was Annie. He had been with women before, but he had never felt the powerful desire to meld his very being with another. Will lowered his hand and spread her legs apart. Finding the tiny nub nestled in its soft cover of hair; he rubbed in a circling motion. Annie let out a loud groan as she felt sensation begin to build. Will continued to caress her sweet spot until a flood of sensation like a Tsunami rode through her body and immersed her on the ocean of ecstasy. Gulping for air, she lay in a haven of bliss. She was floating on the softest cloud in the universe. Opening her eyes, she smiled at Will.

"That was amazing. I feel incredible. I didn't know that such feelings could exist. I never want to leave this place."

"Ah, Annie, my love, there is so much more to the experience"

"More? What else could there be?"

"We have not yet coupled, mo chiall, but I wanted you to experience the joy of love making before going any further. Close your eyes again and relax."

Annie did as Will asked in anticipation of recapturing the feeling of bliss she had experienced a few moments ago. Will made love to her with kisses and caresses, all the while murmuring how much he adored her. This time as the pressure started to build in her lower regions, Will spread her legs farther apart and keeping his passion in check, slowly pushed his penis inside her. She started to stiffen, but then remembered that this was Will and she trusted him. She relaxed again and he pressed a little further. Coming up against her barrier, he gave one powerful thrust and it tore like a curtain dividing the known from the unknown. Annie gave a quick gasp and grabbed both of his arms in pain. Her nails dug deep into his skin and he winced.

"It's okay love. That's all the pain there will be. I have broken your maidenhead and our lovemaking will not hurt again. Let go of my arm. You'll soon experience those wonderful feelings again."

Annie released her grip. Will plunged into her with long, slow thrusts.

"Am I hurting you?"

"No," replied Annie, amazed that she didn't hurt any longer and her body had stretched to accommodate him. Then the pressure started to build again and she lost all conscious thought. The passion built in both of them until they let out a yell and Will collapsed on top of her. The air sizzled with the cry of the union of two souls, who were now intertwined for all of eternity. The auras of the two individuals merged into one glow of purple and gold and the very air shimmered with their love.

Slowly as day turned to night, the couple returned to consciousness. Will removed his penis from Annie's body and rolled over to his side gathering his wife into his arms.

"Annie, we need to get up for a few minutes and clean you up. Breaking your maidenhead causes a small amount of bleeding and I'm sure your legs feel a little sticky."

Annie sat up and looked at herself.

"Oh, will I bleed every time?"

"Just this once. Let me get a wash-cloth."

Will rose from the bed and walked to the washstand. Dipping the wash-cloth into the water and wringing it out, he brought the damp cloth to the bed. Gently he washed his wife's upper thighs and her genitals. She giggled at his ministrations and shyly touched his face. He looked deeply into her eyes and felt himself being aroused again. With a growl, he threw the washcloth on the floor, and reached for his wife. She threw back her head and laughed, all the while pulling him closer to her. Again they kissed long and deep. Once more they journeyed into the land known only to them, yet shared with all lovers that have ever existed. So the first night of their married life continued until finally they both fell asleep, safe and secure in each other's arms.

Victoria broke from her reverie and stared out of the window. "Will, please come home. I long to feel your hands on me again, it's seems an eternity since I saw you last. I can't bear it any longer. Oh, Will." Tears streaming down her cheeks, the spirit vanished into the mists of time.

Chapter Twenty-Nine

*O*nce the building inspector had given his blessing on the house, David and Rebecca put in an offer that was accepted and on June 6th, they became the official owners of Stone Cottage. Driving to their new home away from home they were as excited as two children on Christmas morning. Rebecca went to the herb garden behind the kitchen to start weeding and designing the layout for her new plants. David toured the more formal gardens to set in his mind how he could expand the environs to use as an extension of his business. He worked around the greenhouse, cleaning out the garbage and writing down a shopping list of what he would need for repairs. At lunch, the two met on the old bench by the willow tree to talk about their plans.

"The basic foundation of the greenhouse is intact and most of the glass is good. With a little bit of elbow grease and some minor repairs, I think it will work out fine."

"That's great. I was thinking that maybe we could use this place to supply the company with a greater variety of new plants and shrubs. The herb garden could be expanded and we could sell them in our main store. Perhaps we could plant lavender and have lavender products for sale. There are so many possibilities. For the first time in ages, I am starting to feel excited about something."

"Hmm...is that a convoluted way of asking for a job, Ms. Wainwright?" David laughed. "What about the company and James? Aren't you going back to work there? I thought you loved your job."

"I've been doing a lot of thinking since I got sick. My work with Dr. Holden has made me realize that one of my reasons for hanging onto the company is that I needed to prove to my Dad that I am as capable of holding an executive position as any man. After talking it through with the doctor, I realize that really is distorted thinking. My Dad loved me and that's all I need. I can be whoever or whatever I want to be. If I do decide to go back to Wainwright, and that's not a given, it'll be because I want to, not to prove something. With James it really is his lifeblood. His 'legacy' he called it. For me, not so much. Maybe it's time for a change."

"Wow. I never thought I'd hear you say that. I'd love to have us work together. You have so many great marketing ideas I'd be nuts to turn you down. If you decide to leave, you have a job waiting at Connacher Landscaping, although maybe the first marketing project will be a name change for the company."

***

Climbing into bed later that night, Rebecca picked up a stack of pages from Henrietta's diary. *I wonder if I can find something that showed she had at least a little happiness in her life.* Searching through the writings she came upon an entry dated September 14, 1856.

> I am with child again. Jonathan is overjoyed that Annie will now have a little brother, or sister, to play with so she won't be so lonely. This baby will be MINE and this time it WILL be a boy. I'm sure of it. I will be as close to him as Jonathan is with our daughter. I will have someone of my own that would love and adore me. We will be confidantes and I know

that I will never be lonely again. I
will not make the same mistakes that
I made with Victoria. This time it
will be different. I know things will
be better.

The newspaper clippings said that she did have a
son. I wonder what she wrote about him. Rebecca searched
through the other pages of the diary. She found one dated
May 5, 1857.

He is here! On May 2, 1857 Master
Edward Phillip Smythe-Stratton
made his entrance to this mortal coil,
squalling at the audacity of rough
hands pulling him from his warm and
comfortable sanctuary. He makes me
laugh with his temper. I love him so
much even if he's a red faced,
impatient ball of flesh. Holding him
in my arms feels like heaven. I am so
relieved. The heir has arrived. I have
succeeded. Thank goodness the
marriage act is over. We will have
separate rooms and I can devote my
time to Edward. Just looking at him,
I can feel my heart melt. I actually
feel happy for the first time since I
left Halstead. Maggie is happy for
me. The two of us will spoil this
baby. He will always be loved and
will never know a minute of
loneliness or despair.

She did know some happiness. I'm so glad. Why
didn't it change her? I think I read something at the library
about the baby dying. Maybe that's why. I wonder where
his grave is. He wouldn't be with Victoria as Stone Cottage

came years after he died. Let's see if Henrietta wrote about it. Ah, here we are.

April 15, 1859. My baby is dead - my beautiful, beautiful boy. Love of my life, heart of my hearts. Influenza, they said. Nothing could be done. Was it only a few weeks ago we were laughing and playing together? We were in the garden and he found a bird's nest in the low bushes beside the house. He was so excited.

"Wook, Momma, wook. Birdie."

There were three eggs in the nest and I told him that they had baby birdies in them and that we would watch them hatch. He didn't want to wait.

"Now, Momma, now," he said.

As if I could somehow make them hatch right away. So impatient my little man, he believed I could do anything. Now, who will believe in me? I've told Jonathan that I am taking him to Halstead to be buried with his ancestors. Perhaps I won't return. There is nothing here for me except loneliness and sorrow. Maggie will come with me and we'll find a small cottage. There we will be able to live our lives in peace and solitude. Ah, peace. How I long for it. Jonathan and Victoria won't miss me. They have each other and this is the only home that Victoria remembers. They will be better off without me. My son, my precious

son. How Momma loves you. I wish
I could be with you, my darling boy.

Rebecca put down the pages now wet with her tears.

That poor woman. It wasn't bad enough that she felt shunned all her life, now she'd lost her baby as well. I know she comes back to Canada at some point so I guess she didn't find the peace she wanted back in England. Such a sad life and then to pass it on down to the next generation. I need to be careful that I don't taint my girls' lives. I must find a way to get completely better; if not for myself, then for them.

Returning the pages she'd been reading to the dresser drawer, Rebecca snuggled down under her covers. Thinking about what she'd read and looking deep within her own soul, she drifted off to sleep.

Chapter Thirty

*E*arly next morning, David and Rebecca walked down to the bench by the willow tree. David reached out and took Rebecca in his arms. The two lovers sat each reflecting on the changes that had occurred in their lives. David glanced over at the burial mound.

"Becca, what do you think about the grave?"

"I don't mind it as it makes me feel close to Victoria, but I think most people would find it a little creepy. What do you think?"

"Same as you. When we were making arrangements to buy the place, I did some research and found the McBride family in the small cemetery attached to the old church down the road. There is a gravestone there that lists a William McBride, so I checked and it definitely is our Will. I wrote to the old owners of Stone Cottage to ask if it would be all right if we exhumed the bodies here and buried Annie and Maddy with him. They are the only family left that are still alive and we need their approval before we can do anything. Since the family was separated in life, I'd like to join them in death. They would be together and this spot can be used for laughter and joy again."

"You and Cissy, snooping around old cemeteries," she laughed. "What a great idea. Let's do it before we bring our family to see the property."

Over the next few weeks, David and Rebecca worked long and hard to bring Stone Cottage back to life. The greenhouse was repaired and put in order. A crew was hired to clean out the old carriage house. After clearing the fields, David planted new varieties of greenery including the lavender Rebecca wanted. The herb garden was cleared and pruned. Inside of the house, there was a new coat of paint in all the rooms. Furniture, fixtures and supplies were purchased. They received the go ahead to transfer Victoria and Maddy to lie with William. On the day of the exhumation one of the workers came up to Rebecca.

"Excuse me, Miss. We've found some other bones beside the grave of the lady. What would you like us to do with them?"

"Really? Can you tell what kind of bones they are?"

"Well, ma'am, the crew took a look and we figured they probably belong to a dog. They're wrapped in something. It looks like it might have been a blanket, but there's not much left of it."

Rebecca's senses went on high alert.

"A dog, you say. Were they buried beside Victoria?"

"Yes, Ma'am."

"Well, I presume the animal must have been a dearly loved pet. Why don't you put them with Victoria and we'll bury them altogether at the cemetery."

"Yes, Ma'am. Will do."

The next Sunday, after service, a small gathering met at the Church graveyard where the McBride family was finally reunited.

A few days later Cissy, the twins and Rebecca's Mom drove up to the house and spent a wonderful day exploring the grounds and remarking on the beauty of the property. The girls especially like watching the ducks on the pond and exploring the woods behind the house. Cissy was so happy to see her friend begin to blossom again. When they had a little time all to themselves, Cissy spoke to Rebecca.

"Hey girlfriend, how's it going? Anymore things that go bump in the night?"

"Nope. I'm feeling great. I haven't felt this energetic since before my Dad died. In fact, I'm not sure I have ever felt this awake in my entire life. You were right. The vision of the orchid in the greenhouse was my Dad's way of telling me this place is good for me. I feel whole here. After reading Henrietta's diaries and doing some soul searching, I've decided I want to be happy just being me. I need to make some changes in my life. One of them is to resign from Wainwright and go into business with David. I don't really want to commute back and forth to the city anymore and this seems like a perfect answer."

"Wow, that's a big step. Good for you. Any problems with the exhumation?"

"No. I thought that perhaps something would happen when we moved the bodies, but everything has been fine. Victoria didn't appear like I thought she would. Next week I'm going to come out here for a few days. Feeling the need for a little solitude. Maybe Victoria will talk to me if I'm by myself."

"That sounds like a great idea. If you need me, just call and I'll come out."

"Thanks, girlfriend, but this is something that I have to do on my own. I need to figure out why she's stuck here. Rob said she has unfinished business, but with who? Jonathan? The visions of them when they are together don't suggest there's a problem there. Will? She's definitely waiting for him. Henrietta? There's certainly some animosity there. Did they ever make up before Victoria died? I need some answers if we are to help her."

"Have you thought anymore about a past life regressionist?"

"Yes, I've been rolling it around in my mind. I've done some research but I don't know. Connected in a past life...really? You've talked about reincarnation for years but I've never heard you talk about going to a past life regressionist. Have you ever been to one?"

~ 169 ~

"Not personally, but I do know others that have been. Some say it's helped them a lot to understand their motives in this life. I've never felt the necessity. Maybe it's something we should look into for you, though. It might explain what's been happening. What do you think?"

"We'll see."

"Well, no harm in trying. I'll go with you and stay for the session, if you want. If there's nothing to it, then no loss, no foul, but if there's something you need to know, perhaps this will help us in your search."

"True. Probably nothing will happen and it'll just be a waste of time and money. Maybe I'll give it a try if I can't get Victoria to talk. Dr. Holden suggested that I try new experiences to broaden my horizon. This certainly would qualify. I want to do some more research on past lives, reincarnation and all that stuff before I see a regressionist though. Man, we've had some wild adventures in our lives, but this tops them all."

Chapter Thirty-One

A few nights later, Rebecca tucked the girls in bed and read them a story. Then they sat talking.

"What did you girls think of the new cottage?"

"I love it," they said in unison.

"The woods are really nice," said Amy. "They're dark and quiet. If you sit still you can almost hear the fairies. I want to build a fort in there. Maybe Daddy can help me build a tree house and I can have my own private place. I'd love to stay out all night in a tree house to listen to the quiet and watch the stars."

"Ha," replied Bella. "You'd be scared to bits. If you heard the slightest noise you'd run back to the house in a flash."

"Would not."

"Would too."

"Girls. Bella what do you like about the cottage?"

"I like the pond. I really hope that it will be okay to swim in it and I love watching the ducks as well. Maybe we could get a boat and Daddy can take us out on the water. It's going to be so much fun!"

"I'm really glad you like it because I think we'll be spending a lot more time there. In fact, Mommy is going to stay at the cottage for a few days next week."

"Can we come too?" asked the twins.

"No, my precious girls. Remember how you said you wanted a place of quiet all for yourself, Amy? Well, Mommy needs some time alone for a little while. You know I've been pretty sick since Pop-Pop died. I'm a lot better now, but not quite all better, so I need to go away and think about some things. Okay?"

"No, Mommy, no. We want to come too. Don't you love us anymore?" shouted the twins.

"Yes, yes, my darling girls, I love you to the moon and back. Mommy just needs to be away for a while by herself."

"All right, Mommy," answered Amy. "I understand. We'll take care of Daddy. I'm sorry that you are so sad. I wish we could make it better."

Bella just sat there with her knees drawn up and her arms wrapped around them. She wouldn't look at her mother, her long hair covering her face. She sniffed back tears. Finally, she spoke.

"I'm so sorry if we've been noisy and have upset you Mommy. You don't have to go away. We'll be good, I promise."

"Oh, Bella," cried her Mother. "You haven't upset me. You have both been the best daughters anyone could have. You haven't made me angry or sad. I just want some alone time. I will only be gone for a few days. Next time, I promise, we'll all go as a family. Okay?"

"Okay," said Bella sulkily. "I wish we could go too."

"Soon, my baby girl, soon. Everything will be just fine."

* * *

Rebecca settled into the cottage. During the day, she would tend to the garden, do some research into past lives and write in her journal. Cissy called every day and but as she hadn't seen Victoria, there was nothing to report. One evening, she noticed a thunderstorm approaching from the west. Feeling tired anyway, she decided to go in, have a long, luxurious bath with her new lavender bath salts, read Henrietta's diaries for a while and then go to bed. Soaking in the warm water, the rain playing a rhythmic tune on the roof, she closed her eyes and let the silky liquid caress her limbs. The soft fragrance soothed her tired body. Very faintly, she heard a noise she didn't recognize. It sounded like the soft whine of a dog and it sounded like it was coming from downstairs. Victoria. Rebecca immediately stepped out of the bath, dried herself and put on her bathrobe. She silently made her way down the stairs. Standing in the doorway to the living room, she peered into the room. Illuminated by a flash of lightening, she saw Victoria gazing out the front window. The dog was leaning against her side and whining.

"Victoria."

The woman turned and Rebecca saw tears pouring down her cheeks. Grief had etched deep lines of sorrow on her face. The woman locked eyes with Rebecca.

"Who are you? Why are you in my house?"

"My name is Rebecca and I've come for a visit."

"Did my Mother send you?"

"Why would you think that?"

"She's the only one who calls me Victoria. My Papa and Will both call me Annie, so I assumed you know my Mother."

"No, I'm sorry, I don't know your Mother. Here, why don't we sit down on the sofa and get to know one another? May I call you Annie?"

"I suppose that would be all right. You're the first person that I've visited with in a long time. It's nice. What shall we talk about?"

"Well, you have a very nice dog with you, why don't we start there? What's his name and how did you get him?"

"Oh," laughed Annie. "His name's Thor and I've had him since he was a pup. I was about eight or nine and was feeling very sad after my brother died. My Papa came to my room and said he had something he wanted to show me. He put his finger to his lips like he had a big secret, and motioned me to follow him. We went outside down to the stables. He took my hand and led me to the far stall in the back corner of the barn. There were tiny yelps coming from the enclosure. I looked over the top rail and to my surprise and delight I saw one of Papa's favourite hunting bitches lying on her side, in the hay, surrounded by this mass of wriggling, yelping small bundles of fur. Puppies. I gasped in astonishment. Papa said. 'I thought you might like to see them. Sheba whelped sometime during the night and this is what we found when we came in this morning.' I asked him how many there were. He said there were nine. They were so adorable. I asked Papa if he would be selling them. 'Yes' he said. 'but not for a few weeks.' The he asked if I might like one for my own.

My mouth dropped open, I was so surprised. My heart was fluttering and my body felt all tingly. A puppy! For my very own! I had wanted one for so long, but Momma would never allow it. That thought brought me back with a thud. I told Papa that Momma wouldn't let me keep it. To my surprise, he said, 'Well, this will be a special gift between you and me.' I was to keep the puppy in the barn, but I was in charge of feeding and looking after it. I was so thrilled I ran to my father and flung my arms around him. Never, ever, did I think I would have a dog. I promised Papa that I would look after it and told him how much I loved him.

I'll never forget what he said to me then. He said, 'I know how lonely you are, my sweet. I had so hoped that you would have brothers and sisters for company, but I don't think that's going to happen. I thought perhaps you might like a puppy.'

He had actually noticed how lonely I was. That was one of the happiest days of my life. I went to the stables every day and watched Sheba care for her brood. One of the puppies seemed to be smaller than the rest but fought his bigger brothers and sisters for his place at their mother's teats. He squirmed his way in, around, and under. He pushed, shoved and climbed over the others to find a spot. He was so funny, I laughed at his antics. As the pups started to get bigger, every time I came near the stall, he would come bounding over to the fence, tail wagging, face split into a huge grin and jump up to reach me. I picked him up and he would lavish my face with licks. I knew he was mine and named him Thor, as I thought he was a fearless warrior. When it was time for the puppies to be weaned from their mother, Papa came to the barn to see which dog I had chosen. I showed him Thor. Papa took the puppy and examined him.

'He looks like a grand fellow', he said.

I told him that I loved him to bits.

'What's his name', he asked.

I told him, 'I named him Thor 'cause he's a fierce warrior and my protector' and that's how I got him and he's been with me ever since."

"How did your Mother feel about the dog", asked Rebecca?

"She never noticed him. After Edward died she was more distant than ever. She would rather I had died instead of Edward. I remember when he was sick. Mother was in Edward's room. I had gone upstairs to bring her some lunch. Knocking on the door, I entered the room as quietly as I could.

'What do you want?' she said. 'Please be quiet. I do not want your brother disturbed.'

That upset me, but I didn't say anything. I told her that I had brought her some lunch and I hoped Edward would get better soon.

'Well, just put the tray on the table. I want you to leave as he needs rest and quiet. I think it would be best if Nanny moved you to a room of your own. You are big enough now and Edward does not need you in here upsetting him.'

I was quite shocked as I never would have bothered my brother. I really liked having someone in the room with me at night and Edward was such a happy baby. I loved him very much but no one cared about what I thought or felt. I left the nursery and trudged down to my father's library. I climbed into a chair, curled up under a blanket and fell asleep. Hours later, Papa entered the library and found me in the chair. He walked over to me and stroked my head. I roused sleepily and put my arms around him. He noticed the dried tear stains on my cheeks. He picked me up and cuddled me on his lap. He asked me what was wrong and why I was there. I told him.

'Oh, Papa. Why doesn't Momma love me? Did I do something bad?'

He asked me, 'What makes you think that Sweetheart? Your Mother loves you very much.'

I told him, 'No, she doesn't. Not really. She loves Edward more than me; I'm just in the way.' I told him I was to move to a room of my own so that I don't disturb the baby. I wouldn't do that, but Momma wanted me away from him.

Papa explained that Momma was very worried about Edward right then as he was very, very sick but I told him that she didn't like me even before we had him. She was always so cross with me. Since Edward came she has been a little kinder, but I wondered what would happen if he died. Papa said, 'I don't know, my darling girl. I just don't know.'

Rebecca sat on the couch, her heart breaking for this poor child. She really wasn't much older than the twins and had been through so much in her short life. Annie was so lonely and lost. How could Rebecca get her to move on to her beloved Will and Maddy? She really needed to think about what she had learned tonight.

"Annie, I've really enjoyed talking to you, but I'm very tired. I think I'll go upstairs now and get some sleep. Can we talk again?"

"Oh, yes. I don't remember the last time I went to bed. I don't seem to be very tired. I wonder why that is. Everything seems to be in such a muddle. Do you think that maybe you could help me sort it out?"

"Yes, I'd love to try and help you figure out what's happening. Good night and I'll see you tomorrow."

***

Rebecca climbed into the big brass bed that had been placed into the largest bedroom on the second floor. She picked up the pages from the diaries and decided to read one from before Henrietta immigrated to Canada. *Maybe this will help me understand the woman better.* There was so much animosity between her and Annie that she wondered what it must have been like for Henrietta growing up. She already knew that she had not been prepared for sex. She seemed to be the eldest of the family as she talked of a younger sister, Elizabeth who was supposedly the great family beauty. Rebecca surmised being compared to Elizabeth all the time gave Henrietta a sense of worthlessness. *I would have thought she'd be glad to get away from her family.* Rebecca began reading.

> Well, I have just returned from Halstead. I am so angry. I went to Mother's salon, but unfortunately she was receiving. Ugh, those horrid gossips, Lord and Lady Wistford. Well, it couldn't be helped. I walked into the room. Mother quickly stood and walked briskly towards me. Even though I wasn't expected, decorum must be maintained at all times. Mustn't upset the guests. All she was concerned

about was them. She made polite excuses for my behaviour and we went down the hall to her boudoir. I started to cry. All she could say was 'stop snivelling. It is not at all ladylike. If you have something to tell me, then say so, but without the dramatics, if you please'. I was so ashamed. She can always make me feel so small with just a look or phrase. I took a deep breath and willed myself to hold back the tears. Trying to be as stoic as she is I informed her that Jonathan was making arrangements to emigrate to the colonies...Upper Canada. I said that his family's business required him to oversee a new mill they had purchased and that we will all be leaving in a few months.

All she could say was 'Oh, that's wonderful news but why are you so upset?' Wonderful news? Why was I upset? I was dumbfounded. I couldn't believe my ears. Why wasn't she upset? I told her that I didn't want to go. I begged her to ask Papa to tell him not to go. Did she agree? Oh no. Her daughter and granddaughter were going across an ocean and she would likely never see them again, but did that bother her? All she said was 'My dear, I'm afraid I can't do that. Rathbourne couldn't possibly interfere in a business matter. It's just not done. If family interests call Mr. Smythe-Stratton away, then he must go. As his wife, you are obligated to go with him. I do not understand why you are so upset about this. It's a wonderful new opportunity and frankly, it will be a blessing. It is rather embarrassing introducing him to our friends as our son-in-law.'

I was totally undone! She was glad we were going so she didn't have to be embarrassed. I was furious and said to her, 'I see, it was all right to sell your daughter to him and take his money, but you would prefer not to soil your surroundings with his presence.' To which she replied, 'Henrietta, don't be vulgar.' To be absolutely sure that I understood what she was saying, I told her, 'You do realize that not only will he be going, but Victoria and I as well?'

Then she said, 'Of course you will all be going. Your responsibility is to respect and follow your husband's orders and to take care of your family. I did not raise you to be rebellious.'

I was so angry I could barely hold my tongue. I clenched my fists to try and calm down, but eventually blurted out, 'But, what about me? Have I no say in the matter? I don't want to go to some heathen land and leave all my family and friends.'

I can still hear her response in my head. 'Don't be childish. You are a married woman now and as such, must behave with respectability. You must set a good example for your younger sisters and brother. You are being very selfish. I will miss your company, of course, and little Victoria, but I'm sure that Jonathan will bring you back for a visit in the future. Now, come along and have some tea.'

Have some tea! After she had just dismissed my concerns like one shoos away a fly that is bothersome. Mother and Father won't help me. They had been delighted to marry me off to Jonathan and increase the family coffers, but would prefer not to acknowledge him in front of their esteemed circle of friends. My husband's money enabled them to make an excellent match for Elizabeth. She is to be married within a month to the Marquess of Lindley. Now, there is a son-in-law of whom they can be proud. Jonathan is taking his family across the ocean but that's fine with Mother as she feels it is the perfect solution to an irritating problem. If I have to sacrifice my own happiness for the sake of the family, then so be it. I have always been a dutiful and loving daughter but for the first time I realize that I'm simply a pawn in the game of status that is the ton.

Never have I felt so betrayed. There was no sign of remorse or loss at the thought of me leaving my home and country, possibly for good. No love or compassion shown for how frightened I am. No understanding of what it would do to me to lose everything that is familiar; home, family, friends and country. My heart is completely shattered. I don't know if I'll ever be whole again. I feel a deep penetrating cold inside me. I can feel it slithering around in my belly. It feels like it is weaving a glacial cage around my heart. They are not willing to help me...then so be it. I shall turn my back on them as decisively as they have turned their backs on me. Oh, how I hope that the Marquess of Lindley is a fop! Let their precious Elizabeth suffer as much humiliation and heartache as I do.

Rebecca put down the journal and rubbed her eyes. *Wow, the Countess was a real shrew. No wonder Henrietta was upset, but it still doesn't explain why she disliked Annie so much. I found the entry regarding Edward's birth. I wonder if there is one about Annie's birth.*

Rebecca rummaged through the remaining entries and found an entry dated January 28, 1872.

It's over and the child is here. Darkness, like lava oozing down a mountainside smothering all life in its path, has slithered over my soul destroying all joy and hope. A girl. Now Jonathan will have to put that disgusting rod into my body again until we get a boy. I had so hoped for a boy so that I could heal and perhaps we could learn to be a real family. Jonathan and I could become friends without anything between us. I do not want this child. She reminds me of my failure as a wife and how much I hate what I have to do to conceive. Hopefully she will be a dutiful girl and when she is grown I will be able to marry her off to someone who is worthy of her and I can lose the stigma of being a tradesman's wife and regain my place in society. At least that will be some consolation for the nightmare it took to conceive her.

Putting down the journal, Rebecca picked up her cell and dialed Cissy's number.

"Hey, it's me."

"Hey, you. What's up?"

"I've just had a talk with Victoria. By the way, she's allowed me to call her Annie."

"Do tell. I'm all ears. Lay it on me, sister."

Rebecca then told Cissy all about her encounter. "Then I came up to bed and read two of Henrietta's diary entries from before she came to Canada. Wow. What a family. Talk about dysfunctional. I already told you about how she had been pawned off to Jonathan so that her parents could get their hands on his money to keep their place in society and make a great match for her sister. I know arranged marriages were the norm in the nineteenth century, but to read in their own words how it affected women is awful. One entry reveals how she told her mother about their move and her reaction to the news. Let's just say it wasn't very pleasant for Henrietta. I'm beginning to understand her actions a little better now. No wonder she felt so alone and unloved. It makes me angry that her whole life was ruined by her mother's attitude. Then I found an entry from just after Annie was born. It explains exactly why she didn't want her. From her position, it's entirely understandable, but still awfully sad. I'm going to have another talk with Annie tomorrow. I think I'll bring up Maddy and see what happens."

"Look at you, comfortable talking with ghosts. Wow, that's a paradigm shift if I ever saw one. Who'd a thunk it?"

"Yeah, well, I really don't understand how I'm connected to all this. There's definitely some unfinished business here and it seems to be between Annie and Henrietta, but what that has to do with me, I have no idea."

"Maybe you were a neighbour or Great Aunt or something like that. Have you thought anymore about seeing a regressionist?"

"I don't know, Ciss that really seems weird. I know, I know. It was only a few weeks ago that I didn't believe in ghosts and now I'm talking to them. Crap. I just want to slow things down a bit."

"You thought Rob was going to be weird before you met him, but that turned out all right. Now that you're not afraid anymore, even talking with Annie is okay."

"Yeah, you're right. If I can't figure what's wrong on my own, I'll call Rob and probably make an appointment with who he recommends."

"Sounds like a plan, Stan. Call me tomorrow if you have another chance to talk to Annie. I'd really like to know what happened and why she's stuck on this plane."

"Okay dokey. I'll give you a call. I only hope I have something to tell you."

Chapter Thirty-Two

*T*he next morning, Rebecca took her tea into the front room and sat on the couch. It wasn't long before Thor came to her wagging his tail and butting her hand to be patted.

"Good morning, old boy. Did you have a good sleep?"

"He really likes you."

"Good morning, Annie. How are you today?"

"Is it morning? I seem to have lost track of time. I'm fine, I guess. I really enjoyed our talk yesterday. Do you have time to talk now, or do you have something else you have to do?"

"No, I'm fine. Now would be good. What would you like to talk about?"

"Are you married? Do you have any children?"

"Yes, I am married and I have twin girls, who are ten."

"That's lovely. Do you love your husband?"

"Yes, I do, very much. Why do you ask?"

"I love my Will, but I'm sure that my mother doesn't love my father. I've never been able to figure out why she married him in the first place. I guess she really didn't have any choice. It was an arranged alliance, but that's how most matches are made and people seem to get along okay. I was fortunate that Papa considered my feelings. She seems so unhappy all the time. After Edward died she left us and went back to England. I didn't think she was ever going to come back, but my grandparents didn't want her with them either. I heard her and my Papa talking one night. Apparently, they were embarrassed to have her there without her family and divorce was out of the question. Her friends started to shun her. Even her brother and sisters begged her to leave so as not to upset their lives. Poor Papa. I think he was happy with just the two of us, but he would never admit it or abandon her. So she came back and life went back to being unhappy."

"That's very sad, your poor mother. It seems that no one wants her around, it must be very hard for her to be rejected by everyone."

"Well, it's her own fault. She either snaps at everyone or she is silent and withdrawn. It's impossible to talk to her. Not like my Papa, he's wonderful. He's kind, patient and he really loves me and Maddy too. You should see them together, they have so much fun, giggling and laughing. I hope he'll come and visit soon. Then you could meet him and see what I mean."

"Maddy is your little girl? Tell me about her."

"Yes, she's my baby. Hopefully, next year, we'll have a little sister or brother for her, but Will had better get home soon so that we can start," laughed Annie. "I loved carrying her, although at first I would wake up feeling dizzy and sick to my stomach. I thought I was coming down with something, but I did feel a little better in the afternoon. The same thing happened the next day and the next. I couldn't figure out what was the matter. Will called for Dr. Foote to come and examine me. He listened to all of my symptoms and then asked me 'Mrs. McBride when did you last have your courses?' You know I couldn't remember, so I said to him 'Now that you ask, I do seem to be late this month. I think it was about six weeks ago.' He said, 'Well, my dear, there is nothing wrong with you that nine months won't cure. I am delighted to tell you that you are with child.' I couldn't believe it. I was going to have Will's baby. My very own baby! Once I stopped feeling ill in the morning, I was fine. I remember the night she was born. The wind was howling and there was a fierce winter storm raging outside when Madeleine Sarah McBride made her entrance. We didn't care what the weather was like outside because we were so warm and happy inside."

"Tell me about her."

"She's such a happy baby. We all love her so much. Well, everyone but my Mother. She resents her as much as she does me. I wish we could be closer."

"Do you want to be close to your mother?"

"Of course, what girl wouldn't? I love her, but she makes me so angry. She's missing out on so much. Why, just today Maddy and I went into town for ice cream. It was such a beautiful day. Will was called away for work. He's been gone for a few weeks and I had run out of supplies. I decided to take the trap into town. I wanted to get there before the heat would frazzle us, so I dressed Maddy for the ride. She was so excited to be driving into town with just me and was jumping up and down so much I could scarcely dress her. I told her to hold still and she told me 'Yes, Momma, but I'm so happy. We're going to town. I wuv town. Maybe we could get ice cream. Could we, Momma? Could we?' I laughed. She loves ice cream. I told her 'Only if you are a very good girl and promise me you won't touch anything in the stores, okay?' She reluctantly promised. Then she was off to tell Thor she was going to get ice cream. She gave the dog a big hug and a kiss and ran down the stairs to the ground. She held out her arms and lifting her face to the sun, danced in circles making herself dizzy all the while chanting 'I'm gonna get ice cream. I'm gonna get ice cream'. I just smiled at her. I don't think I've ever been so happy until I married Will and came to live at Stone Cottage. I decided to join Maddy we danced in circles until we were so giddy we fell down. After we stopped spinning Maddy ran to me and I hugged her tight. You know what she said? 'I wuv you, Momma. You're the bestest Momma in the world.' I love her so much."

"Yes, I can see that you do. What happened then? Did you go to town?"

"Oh, yes. It was a glorious day. We sang and laughed the whole way. Maddy constantly pointed out interesting things to see. I'm absolutely amazed at her imagination. She's so full of life." Annie stared off into the distance picturing their buggy ride. "Once we got to town we went to a lot of stores to get what I needed. She was rather impatient and started to squirm and fidget while I talked with the store owners. Finally I took pity on her and asked if she'd like to go and get her ice cream. 'Yes, yes, yes. Will I get chocolate or vanilla, Momma?' I laughed and told her she could have whatever she liked. We walked hand in hand out of the store. Maddy spotted the ice cream store on the other side of the road and...and...darted into the street. Wait, that can't be right. My baby." Annie stood up and started to pace the room twisting her hands in anguish.

"I remember. She didn't see the horse and buggy that were coming down the street. It was going pretty fast. I saw it heading straight for Maddy. I think I screamed. Maddy." Annie broke down in tears, great sobs racking her body. "The driver tried to swerve out of the way, but the back wheel of the cart clipped Maddy in the head and sent her sprawling onto the ground. I ran to her and picked her up. I kept calling her name but she wouldn't open her eyes. There was a large gash on the side of her head and blood was gushing from the wound. Blood, so much blood. I remember there were people around and they tried to take my baby away from me, but I wouldn't let them. I knew she was fine. She just needed to be home in her own bed to rest for a while. Her Papa will be home soon and he'll make everything better. She upstairs sleeping now. I should go, I have to make sure she's all right." Annie vanished.

"Wait. Annie, wait." Rebecca called after the young woman but knew that Annie had gone somewhere that she couldn't follow. At least she now knew what had happened to Maddy and that Annie had witnessed the accident. Tears flowed down Rebecca's cheeks.

That poor girl. My heart aches for her. The love she has for her family is so strong it is literally palpable. I can't let her stay in this agony forever. I must find a way to help her get home to Will, Maddy and happiness.

Chapter Thirty-Three

$\mathcal{R}$ebecca called Cissy. "It's me. I've just had a disturbing chat with Annie and I know what happened to Maddy." Rebecca shared what Annie had said. "That poor child. She witnessed the whole thing, but she refuses to believe Maddy's dead. To her, the baby is sleeping upstairs. She's convinced that once Will gets home he'll make everything right. That's why she's been waiting for so long."

"Oh, Becca, that's so sad. What will you do now?"

"I'm going to try to speak with her again, but I'm not sure she'll come back. She was pretty upset when she left. If she doesn't, I'll have to figure out something else. Would you get the numbers of the regressionists for me? I need to find out how I'm connected to her if I'm going to be able to help."

"Certainly. I'll contact Rob. Give me a call in a couple of days and let me know what you want to do."

"Okay dokey. Talk to you later."

***

When Cissy hung up the phone, she emailed Rob. A few days later she received a reply with a list of names. Rob had written that he highly recommended a Jennifer White as he knew her and had worked with her on other cases. When Becca called, she was able to share the information.

"Hey girlfriend. What's been happening?"

"Hi. It's been three days now and Annie hasn't put in another appearance. David and the girls need me, so I'm leaving today. Did you get any information for me?"

"Yes. The one Rob personally recommends is a Jennifer White. Here's her number. When you're ready, give her a call and set up an appointment. I'll go with you if you want."

"Great. I'll phone her when I get home. While I've been here I've done a lot of reading on past lives and reincarnation. It's really fascinating. I never knew that it had been studied and researched as much as it has. Millions of people and a variety of religions hold the belief and it goes way back into prehistory. Did you know that even some of the early Christians believed in it? Of course, there's a lot of controversy but there are some very interesting documented case studies. I'm beginning to think that there might be something to it."

"I've always found it interesting. As with a lot of things there are some frauds out there, but with all of the stories and studies, I'm inclined to believe in it myself."

"Yeah, after my research, I'm interested to see what this woman has to say. Maybe I do have a past life connection to the ghost. If nothing happens, we'll have to try another tactic. It feels weird to be talking about this and I have no idea what to expect, but I'd like give it a shot. "

"Super. Let me know when you can get an appointment."

"Will do."

Rebecca returned home and placed a call to the number Cissy had given her. She set up an appointment and called Cissy. "Jennifer has an opening Monday at six o'clock. She works out of her home in Whitby. Do you know if there's anything that I need to do before I see her? Anything I need to bring?"

"No, nothing you need to bring, but I would suggest that you don't eat or drink anything with caffeine in it. That way you'll be able to relax better."

"Great. Can you come?"

"Yup. I'll slip away around five thirty and meet you there. I wouldn't miss this for the world."

* * *

On Monday, in the pouring rain, Rebecca set out for Jennifer's house. The windshield wipers were going full blast, but it still was difficult to see in the gloomy mist.

Great. This is encouraging.

Jennifer's practice was in a small remodeled garage at the side of her home. Pulling in to Jennifer's driveway, Rebecca sat in the car for a while, trying to calm her excitement. Her heart had speeded up and her palms were sweating.

I can do this.

She wiped her hands on her jeans, took a drink of water from her ubiquitous water bottle, and with a deep breath, pushed her way out of the car. Splashing through the puddles, she ran to the door. It opened into a small sitting room. There were a few comfortable chairs, some plants, soft lighting and a couple of small tables filled with current magazines like Vitality and Canadian Living and some books. In the side and back walls there were other doors and she could hear soft murmurs coming from behind one of them.

Huh. This looks like a doctor's office, not at all what I expected.

The voice got a little louder and one of the doors opened. A middle aged woman, dressed in cotton dress with a little jacket was speaking into her cell phone. Putting her cell in her pocket, she came into the waiting room. She approached Rebecca with a smile. "Hi. Ms. Wainwright? I'm Jennifer White."

"Hi, please call me Rebecca."

"Okay. How can I help you today?"

Rebecca told her about her experiences with Stone Cottage and what Rob had said when he visited the house. She explained that she was pretty skeptical about going through Jennifer's process, but she needed to find out why she felt connected to that house and the people who had lived there. At this point she was willing to try something out of her comfort zone. "I'm not even sure I can be hypnotized," she said.

"That's okay," responded Jennifer. "A lot of my clients have the same mind set when they first come here. We'll go slowly and I will explain everything before we start so that you are not surprised by what will happen. Shall we get started?"

"I'd like to wait..."

Before Rebecca finished her sentence, the outer door blew open and Cissy walked in.

"You made it. We're just going to start."

After introductions were made, the trio walked through one of the inner doors and into a small room. There were a couple of soft leather chairs along one wall; a table in between them that held a lamp; a small table with a few crystals and a leather recliner in the centre of the room. Jennifer sat in one of the chairs and picked up a clipboard and legal pad. She motioned for Cissy to sit in the other chair and for Rebecca to sit in the recliner.

"Now, I will ask you a few questions just to get us better acquainted. Then you'll push the button on the side of the chair to get it into a comfortable position. I'll cover you with a light blanket, so you're warm and cozy. Close your eyes and listen to my voice. We will go on a small journey to help you to go deeper into yourself, and then I will view scenes throughout your current life. When we have travelled as far as we can in this life, we will try to go back further to see if we can find what is affecting your present circumstances. Is that okay?"

"Yes, that sounds fine."

"Okay, let's get started."

After asking routine health questions and jotting down Rebecca's answers, Jennifer began.

"Please lean back and close your eyes."

Rebecca pushed the recliner into a comfortable position and closed her eyes. The lights in the room were dimmed. As she settled into her snug cocoon, she began to drift as if she was floating on a cloud. She could hear Jennifer's voice leading her on a journey through a forest to a cliff with some steps that led down to the shore of an ocean. As she descended the steps, Rebecca felt herself getting more at ease and drowsier. When she stepped onto the sand, she heard Jennifer's voice come through.

"Rebecca, can you hear me?"

She heard herself respond "Yes" even though her voice sounded far away.

"Good. Now I want you to concentrate on a happy memory from your present life."

Rebecca thought of the day the girls were born. David had been so proud of the twins; he marched around the hospital floor showing them off to anyone who would listen to him. Rebecca actually felt again the joy, pain and love that she had experienced at their birth. The whole scene played out before her and she was amazed as the memories and feelings flooded her body. Jennifer spoke again.

"Let's go back a little further."

Throughout the session, they would travel through many settings that made up Rebecca's life until they reached her ninth birthday. It was a spectacular day. The sun was shining. Her Father was taking a week off work and the whole family was flying to Disney World for a family vacation. She could smell the flowers as she sat on the front steps leading up to her house. Her skin was warm in the sunshine and she could hear the bees buzzing as they gathered their nectar. It was one of the happiest times of her childhood.

"Now, can you travel back to the moment of your birth?"

Rebecca felt herself lift away from her vision then floating down again, but this time she was enclosed in a very small, dark space.

"I am warm and floating in a liquid. The space is tight and very cramped. I've been here for quite a while, but something new is happening. A tremendous pressure is pushing me. The sensation has lightened now. Oh, here it comes again and I'm shifting. I'm definitely being forced down a narrow passageway. The canal expands to let me through. I'm moving again and part of me is out of the channel. There's another push and I don't feel squished anymore. But where am I? I feel strange. I'm not surrounded by liquid any longer. I'm in some kind of encasement that is very heavy. I remember from other births. It's a body and I have just been born onto the earth plane. It's very bright here. After a time in the darkness of the womb, it hurts my eyes. It's also cold. I want to go back into my warm, dark cocoon. There are other people here and they place me on top of my Mother. I can hear her heartbeat again, so I feel safe."

"That's good, Rebecca. Are you okay?"

"Yes, I am fine. I remember before I came that I was not in a human body. I've existed before, but not in this frame. It's a bit jumbled right now, but I was somewhere else and in a different form before I was sheathed in this...this torso."

"Okay. I'd like to go back a little further. Do I have the Soul's permission to take you back into a past incarnation that has affected your return to life this time?"

~ 194 ~

"Yes."

"Good. I want you to go back to where you were before you came to earth as Rebecca. Can you see where you are?"

"I am floating in a mist above the earth. It's very peaceful here and I'm trying to make up my mind whether or not I want to return. I know that I made an agreement to come, but for some reason I'm hesitant."

"Perfect. Let's see if we can go back a little further. I want you to see if you can recall anything about a life that would make you hesitant to come in this time."

"Okay."

"What's happening now?"

"The mist is clearing and I'm in a house. I'm female, but I feel very different. This body is shorter than Rebecca's and heavier. My upper back and jaw are so tight with tension, I can hardly breathe. Clenching my teeth and pursing my lips, I feel rage oozing like lava from every pore. In my hands is a pair of royal-blue gloves which I am clasping so firmly my knuckles are white. There are two long windows in front of me that look out onto the front of the house. Oh my God, I recognize this place! It's Stone Cottage and Victoria is here with Thor. He's growling and she's looking straight at me with anger."

"Can you see who you are?"

"Looking down at my clothes I can see I'm dressed in the attire of the late nineteenth century. I'm wearing a blue travelling cloak that matches the gloves and on my head is a bonnet. That cloak...it's Henrietta's. This is the vision I saw when I took Cissy to the house the first time. Oh my God...I'm wearing that cloak, so I must be Henrietta. Oh crap. Memories are flooding my mind. I am Henrietta and the young woman is my daughter Victoria Anne. That's how we are connected. No wonder I'm drawn to the house. We're arguing about Maddy, she's angry with me for something I have done or said."

~ 195 ~

"It's all right. You will remain calm, you're just an observer. Take a deep breath. That's it. What else do you see?"

"I can feel Henrietta's indignation as she storms out of the house looking for Jonathan. He and a young man are in the barn with the horses. The young man is Will, Victoria's husband. Standing in the doorway, I refuse to enter as it has disgusting and dirty animals. I inform Jonathan that I want to go home. Frowning, he tells me in no uncertain terms that we are staying for the visit as planned as he wants to spend time with his daughter and our new grandchild. Furious with him, I turn and stride back into the house and up to our room slamming the door. He always chooses her. Jealous rage consumes me. Throwing my bonnet and gloves onto the bed, I look in the mirror. The face looking back is the one from my dream and visions. This woman is stern and cold, as if she's made out of marble. Her face displays her negative, vengeful attitude with sharp lines and creases. If there is any warmth in her, it's buried very deep. How could I have been that person? Oh, Victoria, I'm so sorry." Tears slipped from beneath Rebecca's closed eyelids.

Cissy leaped from her chair. "Bring her out. Oh, Becca."

"It's all right, Rebecca," said Jennifer. "These are only shadows of another time. You're here to observe. The feelings you're experiencing are old ones and no longer affect you. Just relax and let them go. Deep breath in, deep breath out. On my count of three, you will relax deeper and be calm. One...two...three. How are you feeling?"

Rebecca gave a deep sigh. "I'm fine. So that's how I'm connected. Why everything felt so familiar. Shit. I didn't expect this."

"Let's move ahead a couple of days. What else do you see?"

"Our carriage is waiting and Jonathan is holding the door open. As I approach the vehicle, I lock eyes with him. Wait a minute...those eyes. I recognize them. Enraged with both he and Victoria, I hadn't really looked closely at him before now. It's Cissy. Jonathan is Cissy. No wonder we've been so close. Before leaving, I look back to see Victoria and her husband standing on the porch. Victoria is holding the baby, and her eyes are pleading with mine to come back inside. The perfect family, even the dog is there. I am so jealous of the love they have I can't see straight. I harden my heart and turn away. Climbing into the carriage, I purposely sit with my back to them. I know I won't see my daughter or my grandchild for a long time, but I don't care. When I receive an apology from her, then I might return. The picture's fading."

"Good. I think that's enough. When you awaken you will not be troubled by anything that you have experienced today. I'm going to leave this lifetime open for now, Rebecca, until we have finished working with it. I will count to four and I want you to slowly return to this lifetime in this room. One, the images from the past are but shadows. Two, once again you are in this time period in earth's reality. Three, you are coming back into this room. Four, you are fully integrated with your body in this lifetime in this place. Okay, open your eyes and lie still for a few minutes until you get your bearings."

Rebecca's eyes fluttered open and she looked around the room. Everything was surreal. She could still feel Henrietta's anger and self-righteousness, but only lightly. It slowly dissipated like the smoke from a dying fire. She became aware of the room and the others in it. She turned her head to Jennifer.

"Holy shit, that was so real. I was Henrietta. The jealousy, the anger, the hatred, it was all inside me feeding my actions. What a bitch! It's hard to believe I was that person, but it's true. No wonder I didn't want to come back.

At least I know why Stone Cottage feels so familiar. Cissy, you were Jonathan. It's unbelievable, but when I looked into his eyes, it was you looking back. I'm blown away."

"If I may make a suggestion, said Jennifer. "You and your friend should really get something to eat. After being in another world, place or time, the body needs to ground again to feel back in place. Food is a perfect way of grounding. Then you should rest. What you have experienced today can be very unsettling and you need to rest to keep your immune system functioning properly, so you don't get sick. You have plenty of time to figure out what this means for your life now and what you can do about it. If you like, I think we should meet again to delve a little deeper into this particular past life. Perhaps a between life review would be appropriate. That lifetime has been left open so that we could investigate a little further. I don't like doing that. Usually we close the life and release the Soul to the Light with love and forgiveness, so that any negative patterns will not be carried forward into this life. I would like to have one more session with you to close that life and seal it."

"I agree. Maybe there's something I could learn to help Victoria, since it's probably my fault she's stuck. I'll send you an email to set up another appointment."

* * *

The tea house in town, 'Have a Cuppa', was located in a quaint Queen Anne home located on the main street. It was painted a baby blue with a wraparound veranda in white. White shutters were on all of the windows with ornamental scroll work above the dormers. Inside the heritage building, the rooms had been renovated to include tables with blue and white linen tablecloths and napkins and Wedgewood china. In summer, there were wicker tables and chairs set up on the veranda.

The ladies arrived at the house and decided to sit in a quiet corner of what once had been the library of the home. After their order of salmon sandwiches on pumpernickel bread with Earl Grey tea had been delivered to the table, Cissy took Rebecca's hands in her own.

"You're like ice. Are you okay?"

"I'm fine. Just in shock. That was the most intense and vivid experience of my life. Like I told Jen, the judgement and arrogance that ravaged Henrietta was all consuming. Looking at my current life, there are similarities between me and Henrietta. What an ass I've been. Smug and disdainful with you and so many others - maybe not to the extent of Henrietta, but hurtful nonetheless. Man, how could you have put up with me all these years?"

Cissy chuckled. "Well, you have been a little hard to put up with at times, but then haven't we all."

"Yeah, but really. I would have gone blithely along my way, never even considering what others felt or knew if my Dad hadn't died. Your ideas of the meaning of life and death were just beneath me somehow and I just laughed at them. It's only because my life exploded that I'm aware of my intolerance. Sorry, Cissy, I had no idea what I was doing."

"Lighten up, sweetheart. From the time I first met you, I knew we were friends for a reason. It just took you a little longer. Will you see Jennifer again?"

"I think so, but I need time to process what I learned today. I question if Henrietta ever softened her attitude. In looking at my temper in this life, maybe not so much. Victoria is so unhappy. With the way I treated her, the baby's accident and everything, I'm not surprised she's still here. If I can discover any way to help her through a regression, I'd like to try. Maybe that's one of the reasons I came back, to help her. Do you think that's even possible?"

"Yes. From what I've read we create a map for our lives before we come here, so that could very well be one of the reasons you've come back now. There's a great book in Jen's waiting room, entitled *Your Soul's Plan* by Robert Schwartz. It's all about planning our lives before we are born. You might want to take a look at it before your next session."

"I didn't notice it, but if it will help me understand any of this I'll get a copy before I see her again. Perhaps I should book another appointment next week. Want to come with me if I do?"

"I wouldn't miss it for the world."

Chapter Thirty-Four

*B*efore Rebecca returned to see Jennifer, she wanted to spend the weekend at the cottage, to absorb what she had learned. Arriving early Saturday morning, she put her things into her bedroom and made a cup of tea. Taking her legal pad and tea to the living room, she sat to write her memories of Henrietta. Since the past life session, she had received snippets of information through her dreams and visions. As she was writing she saw the mist filling the room again. A scene presented itself to her. She saw both Jonathan and Henrietta arrive at the cottage. She felt herself being transported back to that place and time.

***

A carriage arrived at Stone Cottage and Victoria rushed out to greet it. Her father descended. "Papa, I'm so glad you've come. Maddy's been hurt and I need you."

Jonathan looked at his daughter. He could see the too bright gleam in her eyes. Her face was flushed and she could barely contain her nervous energy. "Annie, my girl. How are you feeling?"

"Me...I'm fine. It's Maddy who's been hurt, but the doctor is here and he is looking after her. I'm hoping that Will comes home soon. I've told the doctor and I'll tell you a little secret. We're planning to have another baby next year. Won't that be wonderful? A little brother or sister for Maddy. She's not going to be an only child, like I am. She'll have playmates to love and play with."

"My dear, let's go inside."

Annie turned to greet her mother. "Hello, Mother. If you are coming in, I would ask that you be very quiet. Maddy is sleeping. Please, do not wake her."

She turned on her heel and led the way into the parlour. Mrs. Foote was there and she looked at Jonathan with eyes that spoke volumes of sadness and pain. Wringing her hands, she said, "It's a pleasure to see you again, Mr. and Mrs. Smythe-Stratton, even though it is not the best of circumstances. The doctor is upstairs with the baby. He is quite concerned for the mental health of your daughter. She insists that the child is sleeping and does not recognize she is dead. We need to bury the little one soon or she'll start to stink. Oh, goodness, what are we to do?"

Taking her hand and patting gently, Jonathan spoke. "It's quite all right, Mrs. Foote. The doctor and I will discuss the matter and make a decision today. Thank you for staying with Victoria last night. I am very grateful for your kindness."

"Well, I couldn't leave the poor dear on her own now could I? It was my Christian duty to make sure she was cared for, poor thing. Such a terrible tragedy. I was there, you know. The little one darted out into the road just as a wagon was coming down the street. I heard her mother call to her and the baby had turned back when the wagon wheel clipped her as he drove by. Poor man was so distraught. He tried to swerve but couldn't. He has children of his own, you know, and killing little Maddy has destroyed him. I don't know if he'll ever be able to drive again."

"Thank you again, Mrs. Foote. I'll just go up and see the doctor now, shall I? If you could stay here and look after Mrs. Smythe-Stratton and Victoria, I would be very grateful."

He turned to Annie. "I'm going to go upstairs and peek in at the baby, my sweet. You stay here with your mother and Mrs. Foote. I'll be down as soon as I've talked to the doctor."

Jonathan left the room and the ladies made their way over to the couch to sit down.

"Well, Mother, Papa will soon find out what the doctor says and we can take care of my baby. While we are waiting, would you like a cup of tea?"

"Yes, that would be lovely. Mrs. Foote, would you mind putting the kettle on?" Henrietta asked. "I should like to have a chat with my daughter."

Mrs. Foote left the room and Henrietta picked up Victoria's hand. It was like clasping a small block of ice on a frigid winter's day. Trying to get some warmth back into her daughter's body, she began to rub it between her two hands.

"Victoria, are you sure that Maddy is sleeping?"

Annie snatched her hand away from her Mother and stood up angrily. "What are you saying? Of course she's sleeping. Are you telling me I can't take care of my baby?"

"No, Victoria, that's not what I'm saying at all. You are a good mother, but you need to face the fact that Maddy is not coming back to us."

"NO," she screamed. Picking up her skirts, she ran out of the house and down to the pond. When she reached the willow tree, she slumped against it gasping for breath. Lifting her head, she screamed in agony and crumpled in a heap. Jonathan heard her initial scream and ran after her. He gathered her in his arms and murmured, "My poor baby," while stroking her hair.

The two of them sat there for some time until Jonathan finally coaxed Annie to sit on the bench. He again enfolded her in his arms.

"It was such a lovely day. We were going for ice cream and we were holding hands, skipping down the sidewalk. All of a sudden she wriggled free and ran into the street. I screamed for her to come back, but the wagon was too close. Oh, Papa, she can't be dead. Will is going to be so angry with me for letting our daughter die. No, she is not dead. I won't hear of it. Everything will be all right when Will gets home."

"Will is not going to be angry, Annie. It was an accident, but Maddy is dead and we must bury her."

"She is NOT dead. I won't hear of it. If Will finds out I let her die, he will leave me. I can't let that happen. He'll never forgive me. He adores his baby girl and I would die without him. If you and the doctor want to say she's dead, so be it, but I know she's alive. I don't want to talk about it anymore. You know, this is her favourite place on our whole property. We always come here and I read to her or we make daisy chains. Sometimes, in the spring, we watch the geese with their babies when they first start to swim. It's so funny to see them all march in a straight line behind their Momma. We giggle and laugh at their antics. We will do the same next spring, when she's better."

Annie stood up, shook out her skirt and marched up the hill to the house. Jonathan watched her go, his shoulders slumped; his eyes full of pain. How could he help his little girl? Hands folded in his lap; he sat, staring at the ground. Tears splashed down and sobs wracked his body. For the first time in his life, he had no answers. Usually, he could make decisions in the time it takes to snap your fingers, but not this time. Maddy must be buried quickly, but how would they do it without upsetting Annie? What would become of his daughter? He stood up and slowly made his way back to the house. Dr. Foote and Mrs. Foote were just leaving.

"There you are, Jonathan. Were you able to talk to Annie?"

"Yes, doctor, but she refuses to accept that Maddy has died. We'd better go ahead and have the funeral tomorrow. Annie said that their favourite spot is down by the willow tree near the pond. I'll have some men come from town and dig a small grave there. Once she accepts the truth, she'll have somewhere to sit and watch over her daughter. It's a sad business, sir, a sad business."

"Yes, I agree. We'll be here tomorrow afternoon for the interment. I have given Annie some laudanum and hopefully that will calm her and enable her to rest. Mrs. Foote said she didn't sleep at all last night, but spent her time in Maddy's room singing to her."

While the grave was dug, Mrs. Foote and Henrietta prepared the body for burial and placed it in a small wooden casket.

She is so tiny. She looks just like she's sleeping. Such a beautiful angel.

The ice cage around Henrietta's heart shattered as she gazed at her granddaughter. Pent up despair flooded her body and she was wracked with sobs.

Such a fool, why did I stay away from her love and laughter for so long? My fear and pride has cost me dearly.

Taking firm hold of her emotions, Henrietta straightened her attire and walked to Victoria's room. She tried to coax her daughter to have something to eat, but Victoria turned her back in stony silence, so Henrietta descended the stairs with a heavy heart.

"I'm sorry, Jonathan, she won't come down."

"I know, my dear, I know. What will become of her? We'd best take her home with us until Will comes back. She can't be left on her own. Not like this. Oh, my beautiful girl."

"I have been so wrong. I do love her you know. I was just so angry that she was a girl. I didn't want to have you touch me again, but then we had Edward. I was happy for the first time in ages. When he died, the crushing bitterness I felt towards God and everyone who had ever hurt me encased my heart like the Iron Maiden surrounds a body. The pain I experienced left no room for love or joy, so I returned to England thinking it would save us from anymore heartache, but I was not welcome there and eventually shunned by all of those who at one time had been my friends and family. While isolated in my country house I remembered our life here and I began to fantasize that maybe you did love me, so I decided to come back and try. But when I saw you and Victoria together, I was so jealous, I purposely turned my back on both of you. The worst of it is that in trying to avoid pain, jealousy and hatred have become my constant companions. There is no colour in my life. It's like a gray November day, no leaves on the trees, everything brown and dead. I'm so sorry, Jonathan. I have made such a muddle of our lives."

"Henrietta, we have both made mistakes from the beginning of our courtship. Letting you believe that I married you only to be accepted into upper society was the first of many. I married you because I truly cared for you. When I remember our wedding night, I am so ashamed. What a disaster. You were innocent and inexperienced. I knew how frightened you were. I should have waited to introduce you to the marriage act. If only I had gone slowly. You may even have learned to like it and we could have learned to love each other. Please forgive me for my ineptitude."

"Oh, Jonathan, how foolish we've been. Do you think we can start over and try to salvage something of our marriage?"

"Yes, my dear, I'm sure we can. Let's start by being friends and helping our daughter recover from the loss of her child. You understand what that feels like. Try to show her the empathy you feel over her loss. We'll take it slowly, but I'm sure things will begin to improve."

Day turned to night and there was a huge storm. Henrietta awoke to the sounds of thunder and flashes of lightning. At first she was disoriented, not knowing where she was. Sitting up, she remembered...Victoria. She needed to check on her. She got up and walked to Victoria's room. Peeking in she saw the bed was empty. Running down to Maddy's room, she heard Thor whining and scratching at the front door. Victoria was not in the baby's room. Frantic, she called to her husband.

"Jonathan, Jonathan, wake up. Victoria's missing. I can't find her anywhere."

He roused from an exhausted slumber, sputtered, "What? Victoria's missing?"

"The thunder woke me and I went to check on Victoria, but she was not in her room. Her bed hasn't been slept in. I thought she may be in Maddy's room to feel close to her, but she wasn't there either. Thor's downstairs whining and scratching at the front door. I fear something is very wrong."

Alarmed Jonathan sprang from his bed. He dressed as quickly as possible. "Get me a lantern and I'll go and search for her."

Dashing down the stairs to the larder, Henrietta retrieved a lantern, dressed it and ran out to the hall.

"You stay here. I'll take Thor and search. C'mon Thor, let's find Annie."

***

Opening the front door, they stepped out onto the porch. Rain lashed the buildings. The young tree on the front lawn was bent with the force of the wind. Lightning flashed against the sky and thunder boomed. The storm was directly overhead. Jonathan couldn't see very far through the veil of the rain and fog. Leaning into the wind, man and dog set off to find Victoria. They searched the carriage house and the barn but she was not in either. Walking down the driveway to the road, they found nothing. They struggled back to the hill. A giant flash of lightning lit up the sky. Thor began to bark frantically as he rushed down the hill. During the lightning flash, Jonathan had seen a small mound huddled on top of the freshly dug grave.

"Annie," he screamed racing as fast as he could.

Reaching the plot, he found his daughter unconscious, laying in a heap, clutching handfuls of dirt - as if she had been trying to dig up the grave. Thor was licking her face, trying to wake her up. She was soaked through to her skin and her body was icy cold. Jonathan picked her up and stroked her face all the while muttering sweet endearments. Struggling to his feet, he carried her back to the house. Jonathan conveyed Annie up to her room and stripped off her wet clothes. Henrietta brought warm blankets and towels. They quickly dried her, dressed her in her nightgown, and wrapped her in warm blankets. She remained oblivious to their ministrations. During the night, her body was wracked by a fever so severe she went into convulsions. Her parents stayed with her, trying desperately to reduce the fever by bathing her in cool water. As morning broke, Victoria began to cough, her body shaking as if from chills. Jonathan called to one of the stable boys to get Dr. Foote. He arrived a short time later and examined Annie.

"I'm sorry, Jonathan, but she has pneumonia. I will give her some laudanum to help her body rest, but we need the fever to come down. Keep bathing her in cool water. I don't want to bleed her, but it may be the only chance we have of getting her well. I will return later."

Throughout the day, Henrietta and Jonathan took turns bathing Victoria, but the fever stubbornly refused to abate. Dr. Foote returned and reluctantly bled her hoping to reduce the fever. Even with all of the ministrations, Victoria remained oblivious to the anxiety of those around her. By the next morning she was still feverish and had become delirious. She began to thrash in the bed calling out for Will and Maddy. Alarmed, Jonathan again sent for Dr. Foote. He examined his patient and sadly shook his head.

"I'm sorry, Jonathan, I have no more resources in my arsenal. Even bleeding her last night hasn't helped."

Annie's condition worsened. Her fever did not decrease and her skin felt like dry parchment paper. All day her parents soothed her body with cool water, but the heat would not subside. There were times when she appeared to rest, but soon the thrashing would start again as did the coughing spells. In the evening, Victoria called out in her delirium.

"Will, where are you? I need you, please come home. Maddy. Where's Maddy? Oh yes, she's sleeping. Shhhh...We have to be quiet, can't wake the baby. She needs her rest, 'cause she's not feeling well. Please don't be angry, Will. I didn't mean for her to get sick."

Alarmed, Henrietta ran get Jonathan. He took his daughter in his arms and rocked her, trying to calm her down.

"Shhh, shhh, my pet. Papa's here," he whispered stroking her head and face. "Everything will be fine, I won't leave you."

"Everything will be fine," repeated Annie. "Will is coming home and everything will be fine." Annie closed her eyes and with a smile on her face, took one final breath and slumped in her father's arms. The old dog began to howl.

"Noooo, not Victoria as well!"

Jonathan sat stoically in the chair, rocking his daughter back and forth. Henrietta crumpled at his feet and placed her head on his knee weeping, overwhelmed by the losses they had suffered. When the night finally released its hold on the land and daybreak pushed its way into consciousness, Jonathan rose from the chair and laid his daughter on her bed.

"Come, my dear. We must call Reverend Thomas. We'll lay her beside Maddy down at the pond. I think she'll be happy there, and the two of them will be together in their favourite spot."

Thor remained with his mistress and would not leave the grave. He refused to eat and within days he, too, passed into the next world. Jonathan gently picked him up and carried him to the house. Henrietta retrieved his blanket from Victoria's room and wrapped him in it.

"Such a good boy," she said stroking his head. "He was so loyal to our girl. Oh, poor Will. He's lost his whole family. At least we still have each other, but he's nothing left. How will we tell him?"

"I don't know, my dear. I just don't know. Let's take Thor down to Annie and lay him to rest beside her. He never left her side and I'd like to think he is with her now, if animals are allowed in Heaven. At least he'll still be with her here."

"Yes, it's fitting way to honour his fidelity."

Arms around each other, the couple carried his body down to the willow tree. Henrietta cradled him in her arms. Tears flowed down her cheeks and fell onto his still form. "I've been so wrong and now it's too late. Oh, Jonathan. I've been such a fool."

***

The mist dissolved and Rebecca was back to herself in the parlour, tears flowing freely down her face.

Poor Henrietta. She did start to change, but not soon enough. I wonder how I will be able to continue progressing and help Annie in the process.

"Oh Victoria, now I know why I had to return. You deserve to be reunited with Will and Maddy and I will do everything in my power to help you."

Chapter Thirty-Five

*E*arly in the next week, Rebecca and Cissy returned to Jennifer's office for another session. After greeting each other the trio went into Jen's treatment room and Rebecca settled herself in the chair. Before starting, Rebecca related the vision she had seen at the cottage. After counting down and allowing Rebecca to go into a deep meditative state, Jennifer spoke.

"Rebecca, do we have the higher soul's permission to reveal what you want to know about this life and why you incarnated at this time?"

"Yes."

"Good. Now I want you to go back in time. You are floating in the mist between lives. The mist is clearing. Can you tell me where you are?

"I am at Halstead, my childhood home. Jonathan and I returned to England for good after Victoria's death. My mother had died and my father sent for us. He passed many years ago and my brother became the Earl. He allowed me to stay in the house after Jonathan died, declaring it was his duty, but we are not close and he will be glad to be rid of me."

"Can you see the death scene for Henrietta?"

"Yes."

"What's happening?"

"I'm in my bedroom at Halstead, surrounded by servants. Floating in and out of consciousness, my breathing is laboured. My time is near. I am recalling my life and sadness permeates my soul. Anyone who knew and loved me is long gone. My parents, Jonathan, my children, Maggie...everyone has departed and I alone am left. There are no mourners to regret my passing. It has not been a happy life and I'm glad for it to be over. Victoria Anne...how I long to see her again and beg her forgiveness. There is so much remorse about the way I acted and the people I hurt. The doctor has pronounced me dead and is covering my face with the blanket. My soul is separating from my body and looking back, I can see myself lying on the bed. It's disorienting to no longer have a body, but freeing as well. I am still me only more so expanding until I am everything and everyone. We are all connected in a very real way. There are no words to describe the intimacy of the experience. The pain and misery that I endured as Henrietta is gone and I am at peace."

"This is good. We are now going to close the life of Henrietta. All that was said or done is finished. You no longer have to carry the regrets and anger from that lifetime at the soul level. When you think on your life as Henrietta, it will be with compassion and love for the soul that lived. You will carry no blame or dismay at the person you used to be. It is over. Now you are in the light, what happens next?"

"I am greeted by luminous Beings."

"Who are they?"

"Some of them are family and friends from another time period. Many are from this past life. Others appear to be what we would call angels and guides. There's my Mother and Father...and Jonathan. Edward. Oh, my precious son. Will and Maddy. Maggie. It's so good to be with them again but I don't see Victoria. Everyone is welcoming me home from this incarnation. Even after all that I did to them, there is no anger or animosity towards me, only love. I am bathed in what appears to be a shower of light that restores my original luminance and makes me feel whole again."

"What is happening now?"

"It's time to review this past embodiment to see if I accomplished what I had planned to learn before I incarnated. Although, time is a human concept, so I don't know how long I have been here or how much earth time has passed since I died."

"Tell me what you see and where you are now?"

"A group of us are in a medium sized room. There's a large window on the far wall that looks out over a forest. We are on the third floor of a building. A clear-crystal round table is situated in the centre of the room, with six luminous beings sitting in comfortable chairs surrounding it. There's a seventh chair, but it is empty. Floating above the table is a hologram, but it is just wavy lines. It is like a sparkly sphere rotating in place. I'm sitting in one of the chairs. I don't have a temporal body as I did on earth but my luminous body has taken on the form of Henrietta. We are waiting for someone or something."

"What happens next?"

"The door opens and another tall being steps into the room."

"How are you feeling?"

"I'm happy and at peace. It's so wonderful after the turmoil of my life on earth. The sensation is exquisite; I don't have the words to describe it. The six others are Ascended Masters and Guides from my soul group. I've missed them while I was incarnated as Henrietta."

"What is the group saying?"

"Well, it's not so much as saying, as we are all connected to one another, so one's thoughts are heard by everyone. Sort of like we are cells in a mortal frame, all joined together yet each an individual. As some cells connect to form a hand or a foot, each soul here has a core group that we resonate with best, but all groups are joined to make one body. We can change the form we wish to portray...male, female or androgynous, whatever we want

~ 213 ~

to be at the moment. It's hard to explain. Language can't describe the difference between the ethereal and the physical. As the new being takes its place at the table, she speaks."

"What is she saying? What is the purpose of the gathering?"

"She is Lia, one of my Soul group. She is speaking. 'We want to welcome Henrietta from her journey to the Earth plane. We will call her Henrietta as this is her life review and until it is completed, she needs to remain so. Let's begin.' The hologram is turned on. The wavy lines disappear and I can see a woman with a small baby in her arms. 'This is the moment after the birth of Henrietta. The next thing we will see is her blueprint for this life. Then we will view her story in every detail. After completion, we will discuss if she accomplished the tasks she set out for herself to her satisfaction. When the review is over, choices will be made as to if and when she would like to reincarnate or move on to a different experience in the Universe.'"

"What's happening now?"

"Everyone is watching the hologram that shows my experience as Henrietta. We're all talking and making notes about different scenes. Some parts are very painful for me to watch as I see how my actions hurt others around me and their pain and distress is infused into my being. I am ashamed and my luminosity has dimmed. The last scenes of my death are over and the hologram has turned off. The group is now discussing our assessment."

"What do your Council members do while you are experiencing life on Earth?"

"There are different tasks to do. They can coach a soul with whom I will interact on Earth and ready them for our meeting. Observations on my life choices are noted by those that will be in my Life Review session that will be discussed at that time. Some watched over and guided me. I have done the same for them during the various times they chose to spend on earth and I remained behind. It is enjoyable, fulfilling work and helps the group soul grow."

"What is everyone saying?"

"We are comparing what I designed in my blueprint with the actual results of my life. Lia is talking. 'Henrietta, what was your soul's purpose in designing this life?' I reply that I wished to feel compassion while in human form. For numerous incarnations I have used aggressiveness as a tool to cope when life wasn't going the way I wanted it to and my heart became hardened. One of the main things I desired to accomplish this time was to recall that I am an eternal spirit enrobed for such a short time in human flesh. It's important to me to remember who I am, while experiencing human existence."

Jennifer asks, "You have spoken of designing a blueprint for your life. What do you mean by that?"

"As I understand it from my experience here, after making the decision to reincarnate, we meet with our soul group to discuss various goals to help the soul and others in the group, learn and grow. Sort of like designing the blueprint for a house on Earth. Each room is carefully measured, mapped and then placed on a grid. When the plan is complete, it is put into motion and the house is built. In a soul blueprint, we map each detail of life to make the best possible outcome for that incarnation and for the greatest and highest good of all involved. Just as when the blueprint for a brick and mortar house is drawn and revisions are required due to unforeseen circumstances, lives often needs fine tuning once we are born. What had seemed like a magnificent idea in the planning stage may call for an adjustment on Earth. Earth's atmosphere is very dense and it's a difficult training ground. There may be hardships that were unforeseen. Choices made by others may impact us. Free will is always a factor and wandering from the chosen path is a possibility. Challenges designed could be much harder to do than first imagined, such as my experience as Henrietta and her test in accepting the love of Jonathan and Victoria. Occasionally, a soul will get derailed so completely the blueprint is not followed at all and the soul will need major adjustments when it gets back to its soul group."

"Why did you choose to incarnate into the family you did?

"I wanted to understand the feelings of not being loved, so that I could choose empathy and compassion from a place of understanding. I got caught up with the need of making myself worthy of love. The two souls who chose to incarnate with me as my parents didn't want to play this role because they love me so much. We've been together in other lifetimes. They knew the dangers, but because they understood what I was trying to accomplish and as it also served their soul's purpose, they accepted the roles."

"Is it necessary to invite your family's Higher Selves into the room to discuss the important and very unpopular roles they played in your current lifetime? It is my understanding their task was to assist you in experiencing rejection and they did as you requested."

"No, it isn't necessary for them to be here. I am grateful that they fulfilled the purpose we agreed upon. The anger I held around those roles and that rejection is released."

Rebecca released the anger from her stomach area and filled the area with White Light.

"Do you feel that you accomplished what you wanted to do when you drew your blueprint?"

"No, I don't. Forgetting what I was trying to do and the spiritual being I am, I absorbed the feelings of rejection and became bitter and hateful. The old addiction of arrogance and ego took over. This is a very difficult lesson for me. One I've tried to learn over several lifetimes. Oh well, back to the drawing board."

"Rebecca, how do you feel about your life as Henrietta now?"

"Disheartened, but I understand her actions. Jonathan and Victoria's love was there to assist me in building a life of joy and gratitude from the perspective of knowing enmity and rejection. The love was there, but I was too scared to let it in. I had a choice to reject or accept it. Instead of acceptance, I fell back into the old habits from many lifetimes. It was easier to choose anger and resentment than to change. Around the time that Victoria fell ill I wanted to transform, but it was too little too late. There was some progress though, so maybe this life will be different."

"Rebecca, would you like to continue with Henrietta's experiences or do you wish to close for now and visit another time?"

"I'm feeling very tired, so I've had enough."

Jennifer slowly brought Rebecca back to the room and she lay in the chair for a few moments to catch her bearings.

"That was intense."

"Yes, these sessions can sometimes be very forceful, but enlightening. How do you feel about what unfolded?"

"Incredible. Not like anything I was taught to believe as Rebecca. The teachings I have received regarding the 'judgement' scene were much different. I was expecting that it would be in a courtroom with God as the judge, but in this life review although nothing was hidden, good or bad; there wasn't the air of judgement from the others I expected. There was no fear of eternal punishment for my actions, although seeing and feeling the pain, hurt and rejection my unloving actions caused others was torture for me. You can't hide behind excuses. Your motives are very clear to everyone. I was aware, deep in my soul, every single hurtful sensation I had ever caused.

Their pain radiated through me. It has actually become a part of me. God, it's horrible."

"It's different for everyone. I have been fortunate to participate at numerous past life regressions and they are always unique, suited to the personality of the client. I have yet to see two that are identical although they do all have similar characteristics. There are always luminous beings that form a Grand Council and are connected to the soul in some way as part of their soul group whether as Guardian, Guide, Mentor or Teacher or some other way. With them present, there is a full life review. When the review is complete, the soul is free to rest, heal and explore its options. This could take eons of time as we know it depending on the result of the review. If the soul decides to reincarnate, the group will meet again to decide on a new blueprint where numerous paths are presented and discussed. One is chosen as the best way to fulfill the desired outcome, although alternatives are presented to get them back on course if they get off track. Today we reviewed Henrietta's life. Would you like to return to see what Rebecca designed for this life?"

"Thank you, Jen. Yes, I do want to see what I planned for this life and how it connects with Henrietta's. I think I'll take a little while to process what I have learned today, but I'll be back in touch."

* * *

The two friends walked silently to the car and climbed in.

"Would you like to go and get a cup of tea and talk?"

"No thanks, I'd just like to go home. I want to sit with the information for awhile. It's pretty mind blowing, but deep inside, I know it's real. I'm going to make another appointment with Jen because I would like to see if I can find out why I came back now and what I planned to accomplish this lifetime."

Cissy took Rebecca home. She walked into her bedroom and shut the door. Lying on her bed she pondered her experience of the morning. If what she had encountered was true and she felt it was, then she had planned to come again this time to fulfill her greatest desire to show love, compassion and joy to all beings that she met. She perceived deep darkness in the world and felt helpless to do anything about it. Closing her eyes, she let the pain of rejection settle deep in her body. She felt again the burning in her chest and the tightness in her stomach. Remembering what it felt like to think that she was less than others...to feel abandoned and discarded by those she loved, she determined that whatever was left of this lifetime as Rebecca, she would take that pain and transmute it into love and compassion. She lay in the bedroom for a long time, lost in her thoughts and feelings. When she arose, she walked to the bathroom to take a long, hot shower; a new conviction and purpose settling in her soul. The first thing she would do was make another appointment with Jen to see what her blueprint had been.

Chapter Thirty-Six

A few days later, Jen again welcomed Rebecca and Cissy into her office. After everyone was settled, Jen began to speak.

"Rebecca, we are going to go back to the time before you incarnated into this present life. What do you see?"

"Again I'm in the meeting room, seated around the circular table. I do not know how much time has passed since we were last here, but I am told that it has been over 100 Earth years. Lia is here along with my soul group and others who wish to incarnate with me this time. We are all watching the hologram. I do not resemble Henrietta anymore, but have taken on the physical form of Rebecca. Sort of like trying on a new dress before you buy it. I'm luminous, but wispy or transparent, as if the design is not totally finished. The hologram is showing various scenarios of what could happen to Rebecca as I try to determine which course of action would be best to succeed at what I want to accomplish."

"Can you hear anything that is being said?"

"Some. Everyone is trying to help me design the best way to achieve what I want to do."

"What do you want to do?"

"I am determined to learn the lesson of love, compassion and empathy to others on the Earth plane. The energy is so dense on Earth that I want to help the many other light workers who are here bring a conscious awareness to the planet. To raise the vibration and usher in a higher energy that will dissipate the darkness."

"What is happening now?"

"The being who was Henrietta's Jonathan is talking to me. He is saying that he would like to be with me again this time as he wants to see the task through. We are trying to decide how best to accomplish this. We agree he should be female this time and my best friend. I will be glad to have her with me as we are very close and have similar goals. The plans we make will suit both of our purposes well."

"What else is being discussed with the group?"

"We're talking about Victoria from Henrietta's life and how she is an earthbound spirit."

"What has been said about that?"

"Although the others have assured me that I am not responsible, I feel I am. Victoria's had a lot of help from this side to return home but has refused it. I'm adamant that I need to help her. The others agree that the task is do-able, but I could get lost myself if I try. We are all trying to find a resolution to the problem. It will be tricky to find a way to complete my goals yet help Victoria move on at the same time.'"

"What plans are you making to help Victoria?"

"I'm discussing my ideas with a being named Randal, who is an old soul and part of my group. He's experienced a lot in his many lives and would like to manifest once more to finish up a couple of things before he moves on to other realms. We talk about what role he could play in my life and decide it would be best if he is my father. He will only stay with me for a short while and will leave suddenly. This act will radically change my life and start my search for Victoria. There's the possibility that losing him so suddenly I could fall into the darkness of deep depression, from which I don't recover. This will be a great challenge for me."

"Is there anyone else from Henrietta's life that is with you this time?"

"Yes. Maggie is here. She wants to be on a more equal footing. Because of our master/servant connection in Henrietta's life she feels she couldn't support me in the way she wanted. We agree that the best way for her to help Rebecca is for her to come as my husband, David. We have been in each other's lives many times before and it's always good to have her near."

"Is there anything else of importance that we need to examine at this time?"

"No. We're still discussing other aspects of this life, but I feel that I have seen what I need to learn for now. The room's beginning to fade and the voices are becoming faint."

"That's good, Rebecca. You are now coming back into this room."

As Jennifer brought Rebecca back to this reality, she lay in the chair, silently thinking about what had happened. Tears slipped from her eyelids as she realized how much Randal had loved her and how grateful she was to him for all that he had given to her. She also concluded that Cissy had been right. It was his time. She quietly thanked him in her mind for his gift and wished him well on his next journey.

She got up from the chair and hugged Jennifer. "Thank you so much for all of your help. This was amazing. We're done for now as I have all the information needed to accomplish what I set out to do. I'll be sure to let you know what happens."

"I'm so glad you found what you were looking for and wish you all the best on your journey. I would appreciate you keeping in touch as I'm very interested to find out what happens to Victoria."

Rebecca and Cissy left her office and went to Have a Cuppa. After sitting at their usual table and placing their orders, Rebecca reached out and clasped Cissy's hand.

"Thank you, my friend. I know we've been close for a long time, but I didn't realize how long. Sheesh, if you'd dumped me; I don't know where I'd be. You were right about my Dad. It was his time."

"Naw, I wouldn't leave...after all we've been through? It amazes me that sometimes what we think of as bad things can actually have been for good and for the soul's growth. I know with free will, it doesn't always work that way, like in Henrietta's life, but we're always given a chance to try again. Speaking of Henrietta, what are you going to do about Victoria?"

"I'm not sure, but she needs my help. She doesn't frighten me anymore. I'm going back out to the cottage and I hope she'll talk to me."

Chapter Thirty-Seven

*R*ebecca drove to the cottage just as the sunrise was bathing the stones in pastel luminescence. She stood and gazed lovingly at the house. Contentment welled up in her heart and swept over it like the ocean washing the shore and wiping away all the debris that had collected there throughout the years. Before entering the house, she walked down to the bench. Sitting, she watched the ducks swim on the pond and closed her eyes, letting the sun warm her face with its soft caress.

She thought about all she had learned in the past weeks. How, as Henrietta, she had never appreciated the beauty and love that had sheltered this piece of earth. Looking at where the graves had been, she now saw a lovely lawn sloping down to the pond. She thought about the two lives, one so cherished that when she passed the other sought to follow. How was she going to help Victoria? Would she even appear to her again? She was no longer afraid, for she knew the ghost meant no harm; she was just waiting for her love. Sighing, she rose from the bench and walked back to the house. This time when she entered there was no cold blast, but a warm welcome home. There was no vision of an old grandfather clock, just the solidity of the furniture she and David had placed inside. Entering the front room, no ghost appeared. She would have to be patient. Perhaps Annie would appear tonight. Perhaps not, but she would wait as long as it took. On that she was resolved.

Rebecca stayed at the house for three days, puttering around the garden and cleaning from top to bottom. On the evening of the third day, as she was preparing for bed, she heard the dog whining. Quickly, she descended the stairs and went to the front room. As before, the young woman stood facing the window and looking out at the garden. The dog leaned against her leg.

"Hello, Annie."

Thor ran up to meet her wagging his tail. "Hi there, baby. You're such a good boy. Have you been looking out for your mistress?"

"You came back."

"Yes, I know you're lonely and I wanted to see you again. Will hasn't come home yet?"

"No. Do you know where he is?"

"I haven't seen him, but I do know where he is."

"Where? Why isn't he home? I don't understand."

"I imagine it's very difficult for you."

"Doesn't he know how much I need him?"

"I'm sure he does. It seems like you've been here quite a while. Have you been waiting long?"

"I don't know. Yes...no, I can't remember. It seems like only a few days, but then it seems much longer. I'm very confused."

"Annie, it's been a very long time. Actually, it's been more than a century. I'm here to help you. Will isn't coming home. He has been dead for a long time as have you. It's time for you to go to home, Annie. Will and Maddy are both waiting for you."

"What? No. That can't be right. I am not dead and neither is Maddy. Why are you saying these things? You're trying to confuse me. Go away. I don't want you here."

As Annie got up from the couch she and Thor disappeared. Rebecca sighed.

Shit. That was underwhelming.

She would just have to keep trying. Every day Rebecca watched for Annie to reappear. Whenever she smelled her fragrance or sensed she was near, Rebecca would talk gently to her, hoping that she would materialize.

Sometimes Rebecca would catch a glimpse of the woman and dog, but as soon as she started talking, they would be gone. She was at a loss as to what she should do next.

* * *

Rebecca stood in the master bedroom, her brow creased in a frown. She gazed into the mirror. She could hear Annie downstairs but didn't know how to reach her. How could she convince her that she was dead and that she needed to move into the light? Rebecca had tried everything to get her to listen, but she either put her hands over her ears while she screamed at her to get out of her house or just disappeared. What more could she do? A tiny ball of light appeared in the top left corner of the mirror. As Rebecca gazed at it, the ball grew larger until a ghostly figure appeared over her right shoulder. Rebecca gasped and turned quickly. Her heart was pounding although she should have been used to seeing ghosts by now. The figure was of a woman of her age dressed in the custom of the nineteenth century.

"Henrietta," she gasped.

"Yes," answered the ghost with a smile.

"How can you exist if I am here?"

"I'm only part of you. When you come to this planet in any lifetime, you leave a large part of yourself at Home. I am a fraction of that part. You only bring with you the part that will aid you in accomplishing what you set out in your plan. It is hard to explain. The life we live is just one very small chapter of a much greater whole. It goes by so quickly. The soul is so much more than any one body. Think of a wardrobe in which you have many different outfits. When you have a business appointment, perhaps you choose to put on a classic business suit or a power dress. When you are going to the beach, it may be capris and a top, or something more casual. They are all part of your wardrobe and belong to you; you just don't wear them all at the same time. The same is true of the bodies we inhabit when we come to Earth. You choose a body that will serve you for that lifetime and for the lessons you have chosen to learn. You have had many bodies in many periods throughout time but each one is not the total of the magnificent being that you are. Right now, you inhabit the Rebecca version of the eternal you. I am a past version but I'm still part of you and have been allowed to come as Henrietta to help you with Victoria. She must be released from her state of limbo, to enable her soul to continue on its journey."

"Yes, I remember how every soul is so much more than any one incarnation. I'm glad that you are here to help. I want to repair the hurt that we did."

"You can't undo the damage, but you can learn from it. Have you accomplished what we've been trying to learn through many lifetimes, Rebecca?"

"Yes. All life on earth is precious, and each has their own blueprint. I don't have to prove that I'm right or better than anyone else. I'm not. My intention has always been to treat everyone with love and compassion, recognizing that though we are different, at our core we are all one. This time, I think I've finally got it."

"Well done! You have finally incorporated this lesson at the soul level and it will help us in the next stage of our growth. Now, to help Victoria, I have an idea. If you will permit, I should like to inhabit your body for a while and present us to Victoria as me. I think I can get her to listen to me. You will always be aware that we are two people sharing one body, but we will look like Henrietta. Do you agree?"

"How is that possible?"

"It is like slipping on a cloak. I will join with you. I'm just a piece of you, like a jigsaw puzzle, and our incarnations are but pieces of the whole. You will still be

Rebecca on the inside. Only the outward appearance will change although you will have my memories of my life with Victoria."

Rebecca began to pace the room, while Henrietta stood silently, hands folded in front of her. After thinking it over she looked at Henrietta.

"I agree. Let's do it."

Henrietta moved towards Rebecca. Sliding over her like a silk blanket, she quickly encased Rebecca's body. Rebecca felt an initial shock, but soon it was like putting on an old and favourite sweater. She recalled the feel of Henrietta's body and it was bittersweet to think about the person she used to be. Henrietta's familiar fragrance encompassed her and she was carried back in memory to a time long ago. She moved to the mirror and saw the face of the lady she had been in ages past. It was an odd but not unpleasant feeling to be both Henrietta and Rebecca at the same time. She moved out of the bedroom and down the staircase to the parlour.

Henrietta/Rebecca stood in the open doorway. The room looked as it had in 1875 as Rebecca knew it would. Annie was in her place by the window.

"Victoria," she called softly.

Annie turned. Her hand flew to her mouth and she gasped.

"Mother," she said.

She started to run toward her mother, but then stopped. "Where's Papa," she asked, biting her bottom lip? "I don't need you. I'm waiting for Will and as soon as he arrives, I'll be fine."

"Your father isn't here right now, just me. I came to talk to you. Will you sit with me for a while?"

Annie lifted her chin and walked over to the chesterfield. Thor followed, staying close to her side. Annie sat on the edge of the couch, her back ramrod straight; her mouth closed in a grim line. Thor sat beside her and she placed her hand on his head. Henrietta calmly walked to the sofa and sat down near her daughter.

"Ah, Thor," she said smiling at the dog. "You've been so loyal, haven't you?"

Suspicious, Annie looked at her mother. "You're acting strangely. Since when have you been concerned about Thor? If you are here to tell me to get rid of him again, you're wasting your breath. This is my home and I want him here."

"No, I'm not here to criticize Thor. In fact, I am glad he has been with you all this time as you must get lonely when Will is away. I know I appear different to you, my dear and you're quite right. I have been doing a lot of thinking about you, your father and myself and would like to talk to you about us." She smiled at her only child.

"Well, something is very different. You look happy to see me. You've never done that before except when you were showing me off to your friends. The last I knew there was no 'us', so what do you want to talk about?"

"Victoria, I want you to understand why I've treated you the way I have and to ask your forgiveness. You're a grown woman, so I will speak plainly. When your father and I married it wasn't a love match. Knowing my parents had sold me to him to gain access to his wealth; I did not believe he cared for me. I was a pawn in their negotiations. Arranged marriages were expected, of course, but still, it hurt very much. I felt ashamed and humiliated. Your father was very kind to me but I didn't want to be married at all. I really wanted to be at home with Maggie and my books.

I was a virgin at the time and the marriage act itself frightened me. I knew absolutely nothing. All your grandmother said was to allow anything and it would be over quickly. On our wedding night, I lay in the bed terrified, listening to the sounds of your father's evening toilette and getting more anxious by the moment. When he came to me, my heart was racing so badly I thought I would die. We were never allowed to show any great emotion at home, so I had no reference for what I was experiencing. Jonathan was very gentle but feeling his hands on my body roused intense passion that I didn't know to handle. Telling myself the intimacies were disgusting, I turned away. I knew I had to continue letting him do those things to me until I gave him an heir, so when I conceived I was hoping you would be a boy. When you turned out to be a girl, disappointment so overwhelmed me that I couldn't bear to look at you. I would still have to 'perform my duties', as your grandmother called them.

As you grew a little older, you and your father became very close. You had a bond that I didn't share and I felt left out. He even gave you a pet name. I insisted on calling you Victoria, but he gave you the name Victoria Anne, and then called you 'Annie' as an endearment. No one had ever loved me enough to call me by a pet name. I so wished he would call me 'Etta' or some such thing. The closer you two bonded, the more jealous I felt and the more I took it out on you. Finally, I conceived again and was ecstatic when Edward was born. I had produced the heir. Life would now be perfect. But it was not to be. When he died, all hope went out of me. I couldn't stand to have Jonathan touch me and ran away to England. When I finally did come back, your father thought that I didn't want to be his wife anymore and turned away from me. He lavished more and more love onto you and that drove us even farther apart. Fierce jealousy enraged my heart. I knew it was my fault that our marriage was broken but I didn't know how to fix it."

Annie was dumbfounded at her mother's confession and her mouth formed a small 'o'. Never in a million years would she have thought that Henrietta would admit the problems in her marriage could possibly be her fault. A small part of her remained skeptical and abused. "Go on," she said. "You have my attention."

"I really did want to have a happy family, but as I said, I didn't know how to mend things. Going back to England that last time made me realize there was no life for me there either. Your grandparents were appalled that I wanted to leave you and your father here and stay in England. They said divorce didn't happen in our family. Did I really want to embarrass them that way? How could I be so selfish? And on and on. My friends had all moved on and had their own families. There was no one left who cared for me or who was willing to put me up and risk the scandal that would come. I came back here determined to make a better home life.

Things had changed a lot while I was gone, and though we were civil to one another, I couldn't get past the wall that was between your father and me. The day he notified me that he was giving his permission for you to marry Will, was the last straw. I was furious. Here I was, trying to make things right and you were leaving to marry a man I considered far beneath you in social status. No one was thinking about me and how I would feel. It was unbearable, so I gave you that foolish ultimatum. I'm so sorry. I know now that Will is a fine man and you love him dearly. I cut myself off from you out of spite and feelings of deep betrayal. That was nonsense, of course, but I foolishly let me feelings get in the way of my love for you and I do love you, you know, but I have expressed it very badly - if at all."

Annie was stunned. She listened to every word her mother said and gradually, as Henrietta spoke, she felt her heart begin to melt like a snowman on a warm spring day. Her eyes had been downcast the whole while her mother had been talking. Now she lifted her head and looked her mother in the eye.

"I have never felt your love. It was the one thing I lacked and so desperately wanted. I understand now why you did the things you did, but I have spent my entire life without you and I'm not sure that I can trust this change. I would very much like for us to have some rapport, but don't know if it's possible."

"I understand, Victoria. I do want a loving relationship with you, which is why I am here. Perhaps we can start now?"

"I would like to try, Mother."

"Thank you, my dear. I am very tired and we have talked long enough this evening. I am going up to bed but I'd like to continue our talk in the morning, if that's possible?"

"I'd like that very much. I will be here when you are ready."

Henrietta kissed her daughter and left. Back in the bedroom she separated from Rebecca. "I think that went very well for a start. I know the weariness of human flesh and I could sense that you were tired, so try to sleep and we'll meet again in the morning."

"Thank you, Henrietta. I feel hopeful that our plan is going to work. Perhaps tomorrow we will be able to help her. I am tired, but I don't know if I'll be able to sleep. What a very strange day."

Chapter Thirty-Eight

The next morning, Henrietta and Rebecca joined again and descended the stairs to the parlour.

"Good morning, my dear. How are you today?"

"I'm fine, Mother. Did you sleep well?"

"Yes, I did. How about you?"

"I...I...think so, but all I recall is standing by the window waiting for Will to come home."

"How long have you been waiting, Victoria?"

"I don't know," said Annie softly.

"Does it feel like it's been a while?"

Annie frowned in concentration. When she spoke her voice sounded far away as if she were coming to some realization. "Sometimes it feels like only a day or two. Other times it feels like it's been ages. I don't remember eating or sleeping and no neighbours have visited, which is strange as Maddy is so ill. A woman came a while ago and she's nice. Her name's Rebecca and she's here for a visit. She told me some things that have made me angry, so I'm not talking to her anymore. I wish Will would come home."

"What did she say?"

"That Maddy and Will were dead. She tried to tell me I was dead too, but that's ridiculous. I would know if I were dead or not, wouldn't I, Mother?"

"I would think so, but occasionally it can get a little muddled. Is there anything else happening that seems different?"

"Sometimes I see a very bright light near me. I feel like it wants to draw me into it, but I can't do that as I have to wait for Will. I won't even look at it properly. As soon as it appears, I close my eyes until it goes away."

"What will you do if Will doesn't return, Victoria?"

"What do you mean? Of course he'll come home. He loves us and he can make Maddy better."

"Will is already with Maddy, and she is better. They are both in the light and you need to go to them."

"Mother, what are you talking about? You're not making any sense."

"Sweetheart, Rebecca was right. Will and Maddy are both dead...as are you. Unfortunately, your spirit has been trapped here because of your grief and guilt and you haven't been able to move on. You have been earthbound for over one hundred years. Will is not angry with you at all, but is waiting for you in the light. He doesn't blame you for Maddy's death. Thor has passed as well, and he chose to stay with you so that you wouldn't be so lonely."

"What nonsense is this," screamed Annie? "Are you trying to make me upset? I thought you wanted to make things better between us. Don't be ridiculous. Maddy is upstairs and Will is on his way home."

"No they're not. Think back, Victoria. What is the last thing you remember?"

"It's dark and there's a storm. I went to Maddy's room to make sure that she isn't frightened. She doesn't like storms and usually comes into my bed. We snuggle and laugh and it makes her feel better. When I get to her room, she's not in her bed. I am wondering where she is. No. No...that can't be right."

"What do you remember?"

"Papa and the doctor, they told me Maddy's dead and they buried her today. She can't be in that cold grave. She doesn't like the cold and the dark. I have to get her. I ran down to the grave and try to dig it up, but it's so wet. I don't have anything to dig with. I tried to use my hands, but they are so cold. I can't get to her. No. No. Our precious baby girl, I let her die."

As Annie's sobs come from deep within her soul Henrietta gathered her into her arms. "Victoria, it's not your fault any more than it was my fault when Edward died. It was a terrible accident. Will was never angry with you. He loves you. The light is here. Can you see it now, Victoria?"

"Yes, but I'm not going to look at it."

"Please look at it, darling. You will see both Will and Maddy are there. Aren't you tired of waiting?"

"Yes, Momma. I'm so very tired of waiting. Perhaps I should look." Grudgingly, she lifted her head and peered at the glowing sphere. As she did so, her eyes widened, her face began to shine and her lips curved into a beautiful smile. "Momma," she said in wonder. "You are right, I see them! Will, Maddy, Papa and Edward are in the light. They are smiling at us and holding out their arms, but why are you here and not with them?"

"I was but I was allowed to come back to get you so that we could all be together. It's time for us to leave. Will you take my hand? Shall we enter the light together and be with our family again?"

"Oh, yes, Momma," Annie replied, jumping up from the sofa. Thor leapt and barked with joy. He ran to the light where Maddy threw her arms around him and buried her head in his soft fur.

Taking the hand of her daughter, Henrietta slowly extracted herself from Rebecca's body and the two walked towards the intense white light that flooded the corner of the room. As they neared the light, Henrietta turned and sought out Rebecca. "Thank you," she said. "When you chose to follow your heart, you helped us grow in love and compassion. You have also freed a tired spirit from its earthly bondage and balanced the hurt that I caused. Stay the course and have a happy life for both of us."

Rebecca nodded in agreement and watched through eyes awash in tears as the two women entered the light and were joined with their family. Just as she was about to turn away, a man carrying a pink orchid entered the light. Her heart skipped a beat and her hand came to her mouth. "Daddy," she cried out in amazement.

Her father smiled at her, blew her a kiss and held out the orchid to her. As she watched, the orchid disappeared from his hand only to reappear in hers. She gazed at her wondrous gift and then back to her father. He gave her a wave and disappeared from view.

"Oh Daddy, I miss you so much. I love you."

Burying her face in the orchid, she shed the last of her tears. As the light slowly faded from the room, she walked to the window and gazed at the front lawn. Her mind felt at peace and she knew without a doubt that she was healed. Better than healed, better than she had ever been in her life.

She looked down at the orchid and smiled. Cissy had been right all along. There was more to this journey called life than she had ever imagined. She really was an eternal soul who had chosen to come to this planet in a human body for a short time. She would be reunited with her beloved father when she had completed what she had come to experience. Annie was Home. Never again would she stand at this window longing for Will's return. Both Annie and she were free. Soon she would be back into the hustle and bustle of her daily routine, but for now, she stood quietly, at the window, cherishing the joy, peace and love of the moment. She sent thoughts of love and happiness to Annie and Henrietta and felt the deep contentment that healing brings. Theirs had been a long, winding journey, but, at last, their paths had come full circle and the journey was complete.

Chapter Thirty-Nine

After Annie had gone Home, Rebecca wandered down to the bench. She sat gazing out to the still water, reflecting on what had just happened. While in contemplation she became aware that there was still a lingering sadness to this part of the property. Puzzled she reached in her pocket for her cell and called Cissy.

She told her all that had transpired that morning and explained that she was now sitting on the bench by the pond.

"I'm a bit confused as I can still feel a lingering sense of sadness here. Annie has returned Home and is with Will, so shouldn't it be all gone now?"

"You would think that would be true, but don't forget there was a grave there for over a hundred years and that's also the place that Annie completely lost her mind when she was found lying on Maddy's burial mound. There is bound to be sadness in the energy of the land even though Annie is safe."

"What can we do to clear it?"

"I'll call a friend, who's done many such clearings before. Let me give her a call and I'll get right back to you."

They hung up the phone and Rebecca sat waiting for Cissy's call. A clearing; another new experience. After all she'd been through, Rebecca knew instinctively this was the next step. The phone rang.

"Nat says she would love to help us. She'll be free tomorrow morning around ten. Is that a good time for you?"

"Perfect. I'll call David, I think he may want to be here as well. Could you pick him up?"

"Sure. See you then. I'm sure that this will take care of any lingering residue from that time period."

***

As arranged, the group arrived at Stone Cottage. Introductions were made and they proceeded down the hill.

Nat said that she needed to walk the whole area with her dowsing rods to find the spots with the heaviest dark energy. After walking a grid of the property from the tree to the pond, she came back to the group sitting on the bench.

"There are still some shadows but they're not particularly strong. I'm sure we'll be able to disperse them in a single cleansing. The darkest energy is there," she said pointing to where the graves had been.

"Ah," said Rebecca. "That's where Annie, Maddy and Thor were buried. They have all moved on now."

"That would explain why the imprint is not as heavy as it should be where a tragedy has taken place. The closer I got to the pond and the farther from the gravesite, the energy was lighter and happier, so this place has known great joy as well. Let's get rid of this dark matter and bring it into the light as well."

Nat laid out her altar cloth on the ground. She retrieved her bowl, smudge and feather from her medicine bag and placed them on the altar. The participants stood in a circle. She cast a ring of protection around the group. After lighting the smudge, she honoured the four directions, the above, the below and the Great Mystery. After smudging all of the participants, she invited the spiritual guides, animals and angels who wanted to participate to join their circle. She smudged the area of the site where the graves had been.

"Great Mystery we are thankful that Annie, Maddy and Thor have found their way Home. We ask that all lingering darkness from any and all of their lifetimes, past present and future be lifted from this place and transmuted into the light. We open our hearts in gratitude for your love. We thank you that our request has been answered. So it is done. Ho."

The group responded, "Ho."

"I now ask all of us to join hands and picture the darkness lifting from this place and turning to the light."

The group held hands and waited in silence. Rebecca could see the light changing and in front of her she saw Will, Annie and Maddy as they had been before the accident.

"Papa, Papa, catch me, catch me," cried Maddy.

Will made a growl in his throat and started to chase his daughter. Thor raced after them barking and leaping into the air. Annie lay on a blanket beneath the tree and looked up from her book. She smiled and her heart was filled with love for her family. Will caught his daughter and lifted her high above his head. Her squeals of happiness echoed across the pond and startled the family of geese that were there.

"Becca, Becca, are you all right?"

The image faded and Rebecca was brought back to the present. Tears of joy streamed from her eyes and onto the ground. She explained what she had seen.

"That's wonderful," said Nat. "The darkness is gone and the light has returned. Thank you for letting me be part of this celebration. I love it when things are put into balance."

After thanking Great Mystery and their spiritual friends for being there, she opened the circle. She did a little happy dance around the group. Everyone laughed and joined her. Soon the small valley was once again ringing with gaiety and laughter. The shadows of the past were gone and a renewed energy of light and love blanketed the area.

Epilogue

$\mathcal{T}$he sunset was a beautiful warm glow of purple, orange, red and yellow. The air was still as the frogs began their nightly chorus. David and Rebecca made their way down to the bench by the pond. So much had happened since the day that Annie had gone home to be with her family and the property had once again shone with light.

David spent some time building the tree house Amy wanted. Contrary to Bella's dire predictions, she did manage to spend the whole night in her sanctuary, although she was back in the house a little bit earlier than usual for breakfast. The pond had proved clean enough for swimming and Bella was beside herself with joy to be able to practice every day for the swim team at school. David built a raft and put it in the middle of the lake where they spent many a day lounging in the summer sun.

After thinking long and hard on the subject; discussing it with James, David and Cissy; Rebecca had resigned from her position as Executive VP of Wainwright Industries. She no longer needed her Father's approval for her work as she knew that he loved her no matter what she did. She thought James was probably relieved to have the company to himself and she was glad to let him take over. She loved Stone Cottage and decided that she wanted to pursue her career working with David. To build a business of her own with the husband, flowers and plants she loved. David was enthusiastic about their partnership and the new ideas his wife brought to the company. Rebecca felt that it would also give her the time and opportunity to work on a new project she had conjured up. To honour Thor and his loyalty to Annie, she was working with the local dog rescue organization to help heal and rehabilitate dogs that had been abused or neglected. Stone Cottage became 'Thor's

Sanctuary' where she fostered many animals in need of love and nurturing. She was happier than she had ever been in her life and was grateful for all of her experiences.

David wrapped Rebecca in his loving arms and spread a light blanket over their knees. "I'm so glad you are well, darling. I've missed you," he said kissing her brow lightly.

"It feels so good to be me again. I still may need my meds to balance my system, but that's okay. I realize now that I am not this physical body and it's all right if it needs some support to help me do what I want to do. You have been my rock and I love you so much. What an amazing experience, but I wouldn't have missed it for the world. I know that life goes on and that death is really an illusion. My Dad is fine and I'll see him again. I understand who I am, have been and why I'm here. It's incredible. Everything Cissy has tried to tell me for years is true. I'm so happy. And this place, I know you were sceptical at first but you stood by me even when my ideas seemed out of whack. I am the luckiest wife in the world."

She turned her head and kissed him in a deep, passionate kiss that had their senses tingling and heat rising in their bodies.

"My darling, you are my 'Annie' and I understand how she didn't want to leave without Will. I never want to leave you."

As they snuggled on the bench, a small, soft blue light appeared in front of them. It was sparkling and began to grow in size. In the light, there appeared four figures. As they projected more fully, David and Rebecca could see a man, woman, a little girl and a dog. All were smiling and waving at them. The man had his arms about the woman and the small child was in the man's arms. The dog was leaning against the woman's legs.

"Will, Annie, Maddy and Thor. Look, David?"

"My God...I do see them."

"Look, Annie and Maddy are blowing us kisses. She's saying thank you. Listen to Thor bark. Oh, I'm so glad you're here to experience this with me. They are so happy."

As they watched the light slowly began to fade and disappear. David and Rebecca sat for a long while letting the shared experience envelop them and bring them peace.

"That was the most amazing thing I have ever seen. Becca, it's true. It blows my mind."

"Yes, my love, 'there are more things in Heaven and Earth, Horatio, than are dreamt of in your philosophy'. These last few months I have spent a lot of time among the dead that I now realize how precious this life is. Make love to me, David. Let's renew the energy of this special place and make it truly ours.

David spread the blanket on the grass under the tree. He reached up and pulled Rebecca into his arms. He kissed the top of her head. She raised her eyes and looked at him. They were shining. He kissed her forehead and slowly trailed soft kisses down the side of her face to her ear. He captured her ear lobe in his lips and began to suckle. Rebecca gasped. He raised his head to look at her. Her eyes had gone dark with passion. Deep inside her body the great need to experience life and passion was uncoiling like a rising snake. Her throat raw and dry, she could see the water to quench that thirst, but she couldn't get there. David. Only David could bring the relief she needed. She clung to him.

"Make love to me, David," she whispered.

David lay her down on the grass and began to caress, kiss and reawaken each precious spot that had brought pleasure to them both over the years. Never had he wanted to please his wife more than now. Rebecca responded with a growing frenzy, covering him with kisses. She was throbbing with need, her every nerve sizzling in anticipation.

"Now, take me now!"

David rose over and entered her. The rising crescendo began in her belly, moving up her body and building to a pinnacle.

"Yes, yes, oh yes," she cried.

Like a mother giving birth, new life gushed from her being in a sensation of joy and completeness. A feeling of merging with the oneness of All That Is. The wave took her to a place where there was no pain, grief, anger or loss. She remained oblivious to anything but the glorious awareness of ecstasy until David cried out his own release and collapsed on top of her. She reached out to her husband and clung to him as if she would never let him go.

"Hold me, David. Please hold me."

David encircled his wife in his arms, and pulled her close. He kissed her eyes, her head, and her ear, all the while whispering endearments. She was enfolded in true love, a constant even beyond time. She realized it was the only thing that truly mattered. Part of a universal love that existed in everything, she was truly free to be her authentic self and to show this love to all she met. She closed her eyes and with a smile on her face, drifted into a dreamless sleep.

Acknowledgements

This book could never have been completed without the expertise of the following: Kevin Whitaker, Carolyn McDermott, Susannah Edwards, The staff at the Whitby Public Library Archives and the Pickering Village Museum, and the numerous teachers who have helped me on my journey. I also wish to thank my Editor, Mark Iles for his hard work in helping me sculpt the final manuscript. Special thanks to Robert Schwartz, author of *Your Soul's Plan* and Rev. Corbie Mitleid for the inspiration for the book.

About the author

Maighread MacKay is an author and visual artist from Ontario, Canada. She is a member of the Writer's Community of Durham Region (WCDR), and the PRAC (Pine Ridge Arts Council).

Her publishing credits include three books for children: Bedtime Treasures, The Mysterious Door and the Crystal Grove written under the name of Margaret Hefferman. Stone Cottage is her first foray into adult literature to be published in 2015 by Solstice Shadows Publishing. She will be included in the 2015 *Christmas Soup for the Soul: Merry Christmas* edition with her story "Being Santa". A variety of magazines have published her work, including most recently, the Durham Region online magazine – More 2 Life 4 Women and the WCDR publication Word Weaver.

Website: www.mhefferman.ca

FB: facebook.com/maighreadmackay

Twitter: @maighreadmackay

Youtube: www.youtube.com/watch?v=RsDj938kUzM

For more titles like this one, visit us online:

www.solsticepublishing.com

CPSIA information can be obtained at www.ICGtesting.com
Printed in the USA
LVOW01s1959160915

454381LV00040BA/884/P